'We could  **and me. N**
know abou

Kieran was s... Just when Jude thought he was going to refuse, he said softly, 'I thought we were just doing friendship?'

'We were. But...' She took a deep breath. 'It's not enough for me. Not now.'

'Me neither,' he admitted. 'But you said you didn't do affairs.'

'There's a first time for everything.' She bit her lip. 'And if I don't, I think I'm going to spontaneously combust in the middle of the ward.'

'Mmm, and we can't have that, can we?'

He was looking at her mouth. She shook her head. 'Stop it.'

'Why?'

'Because...' Because she knew he was thinking about kissing her.

Dear Reader

I was planning my next book when three doctors leaped into my head and hijacked me! Zoe, Judith and Holly trained together, are best friends, and work together at LONDON CITY GENERAL.

Zoe's the clever one, a real high-flyer who's never found love. Until she meets gorgeous Brad, on secondment to Paediatrics from California. Can she heal his broken heart—and can he help her feel less haunted by the secret she hasn't even told her best friends?

Judith's the glamorous one, who delivers babies by day and sings at hospital fundraisers at night. She falls in love with Kieran, the new maternity consultant. But after a discovery threatens to tear their love apart, can she teach him to believe in her—and in himself?

Holly's the 'prickly' one with a soft heart—but it'll take a special man to get close enough to find out! She chose the fast-paced life of the Emergency Department to help her forget her lost love. But when David walks into her life again, will it be second time lucky?

The best bit about working on a trilogy was that I didn't have to say goodbye to my characters. They made appearances in each other's stories! I loved being able to explore a hospital's community and see how different departments work together, and I hope you enjoy life in the fast lane at London City General as much as I did.

With love

Kate Hardy

THE BABY DOCTOR'S DESIRE

BY
KATE HARDY

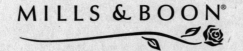

MILLS & BOON®

For Ali, with love

First published in Great Britain 2004
Paperback edition 2005
Harlequin Mills & Boon Limited,
Eton House, 18-24 Paradise Road, Richmond, Surrey TW9 1SR

© Pamela Brooks 2004

ISBN 0 263 84288 6

Set in Times Roman 10½ on 11½ pt.
03-0205-49032

Printed and bound in Spain
by Litografía Rosés, S.A., Barcelona

CHAPTER ONE

'TESS, it's going to be OK. Really it is.'

'But Charlie's been sick over your new suit! And...' Tess broke into sobs.

Kieran held her close and stroked her hair. Why had his nephew had to bring his milk up over him *today*, of all days? After clearing up, Kieran was already ten minutes late for his shift—and he hadn't even left the house yet!

How to make a good impression on your first day as consultant. Not.

But his little sister didn't need to know that. After the junk life had thrown at her this past month, she could do without the extra stress. Besides, big brothers were supposed to be protective, not needing a fuss made of themselves. He forced himself to breathe normally, and hoped Tess couldn't tell that he was only pretending to be calm. 'Hey. I'd better make tracks.'

'But your suit?'

'It's OK. I've sponged it off. And nobody's going to notice baby sick under my white coat. If they do...' He shrugged. 'I work on a maternity ward, remember. Babies are sick over us all the time.'

'Really?' Tess gazed at him from red, swollen eyes.

'Really.' He dropped a kiss on her forehead. 'Go and have a shower. Don't worry about Charlie, I've changed him and I've put the light show on in his cot and he's got his soft book and a teddy, so he'll be fine for a few minutes. You've got your mum and baby group this morning, haven't you?'

Tess made a face. 'It's going to be horrible. All they'll talk about is babies.'

'Of course it won't be horrible. And, yes, they'll talk about babies at first because that's what you've all got in common. But once you break the ice and get to know each other, it'll be fine.' He pulled a face at her. 'Guess what? All they'll talk to *me* about this morning is babies, too.'

'Yes. I suppose.' She gave him a wobbly smile, and Kieran felt the tension in his stomach begin to uncoil again. She was going to be OK. He almost—almost—asked her if she'd try to remember to put the washing machine on. But that would start another discussion and he really, really didn't have time. It'd be quicker to do it himself, after his shift.

'See you later, kiddo. I'd better go,' he said.

The moment he was out of sight, he rang the hospital. He was put through to the obstetric director's secretary and explained he'd been delayed but was on his way in.

And because he'd waited to make the call, he missed the next tube train and had to wait. Funny how his watch was working on a different timescale from the clock at the station: the second hand was racing round his watch, reminding him just how late he was going to be, but the station clock still insisted the next train would be in four minutes.

It seemed like for ever before he managed to get to London City General. He didn't bother waiting for the lifts. If they were anything like the ones at his old hospital, it'd be lunchtime before he started his shift. As it was…

He made it. Forty-five minutes late. Briefcase in locker, white coat on—hmm, he still smelled suspiciously of baby sick but never mind. Chances were, nobody would comment. Not to his face. And he could ignore anything said behind his back. He was old enough and tough enough.

He was on his way to the obstetric director's office when he saw her. The most beautiful woman he'd ever set eyes on. She was sitting on the edge of a desk, talking to one of the midwives—she couldn't work in the maternity unit, then, or she'd be in the middle of a round or with one of the mums. She clearly wasn't pregnant and was wearing a white coat, so the odds were she was staff on a different ward. Paediatrics, most likely. She was tall—not far off six feet, he guessed—with legs up to her armpits. Her red hair was pinned back in a neat knot at her nape, but it would drop like silk to her shoulders if she loosened it. She had a beautiful clear, creamy complexion, blue eyes that crinkled at the corners as she smiled and a mouth that made his knees go weak.

Even weaker when she threw her head back to laugh, and he saw the line of her throat. He wanted to stride over there, grab her and kiss a necklace round it.

Oh, hell. This was a complication he didn't need right now. Until Tess was back on an even keel, he couldn't possibly think about a relationship. Or even lust after someone in secret. Tess needed help to sort her life out, and right now he was the only one who could give her that help.

Besides, the redhead had to be spoken for. No way could a woman that beautiful be single. And no way was he going to be responsible for breaking up a relationship. So he'd better keep his eyes to himself.

He shook himself, turned away from the redhead and knocked on the consultant's door.

'Ah, Mr Bailey. Come in,' Arabella Hunter said.

'I'm sorry I'm late, Miss Hunter,' he said. 'I'll stay late to make up the time.'

'At least you had the manners to call my secretary. I appreciate that.' She gestured to the chair in front of her desk. 'Sit down. And it's Bella. We work on first-name terms on this ward.'

'Bella,' he repeated dutifully.

'And you're Kieran, yes?'

He nodded.

'Good. I've rostered you with Judith Powell today—she's one of our registrars. She'll introduce you to everyone.' Bella rolled her eyes. 'I would have taken you round myself, but I've got a meeting with the trust directors in five minutes. Jude'll look after you, though.'

'Powell?'

He only realised he'd spoken aloud when Bella nodded. 'Yes, she's Ben's daughter. She's a nice girl.'

Professor Ben Powell was the obstetric director at Hampstead Free—the hospital where Kieran had worked until last Friday.

'She didn't want to work for her father, so he had a word with me.'

Oh, great. His first day as consultant here, and he'd be working with a makeweight, a woman who'd got the job because of who her father was. So he'd be doing double the work here as well as at home.

He forced a smile to his face. 'I look forward to meeting her.'

'Come along, then.' Bella ushered him out of the office. And took him straight to the redhead, who was still chatting at the midwives' station.

'Jude, this is Kieran Bailey, our new consultant. Look after him for me, will you, sweetie?'

'Course I will, Bella.'

The gorgeous redhead—the one who was chatting, not working—was the professor's daughter?

She was going to be working with him?

She slid off the desk and Kieran discovered that she was just as tall as he'd guessed. Five feet eleven, so she barely had to tip her head back to look into his eyes. And her voice was incredibly sexy. Low, deep, a little husky. Like melted chocolate.

He definitely shouldn't have thought of that. Because now he had another image in his mind: himself, trailing melted chocolate across her creamy skin and then licking it off.

Stop it. You're a professional, not a sex-crazed lunatic, he reminded himself.

'Welcome to the ward.' Her eyelashes were long. And dark—which meant they were either dyed or mascaraed. But she didn't wear a scrap of any other make-up. Didn't need to.

Stop it. Focus.

'I'm Judith Powell—Jude to my friends.' She held her hand out.

He took it.

Hell and double hell.

Shaking hands was meant to be an ordinary, everyday occurrence. It wasn't supposed to feel as if an earthquake had just hit him. His skin wasn't supposed to tingle like this.

'Kieran Bailey.'

Stupid. She knew that already—Bella had told her his name. But for the life of him, he couldn't think of anything else to say. His mind had gone completely blank, and his mouth felt as if he'd been eating sand. Anyone would think he was a teenager, not a well-balanced thirty-two-year-old.

'We usually do a ward round about now. So I'll introduce you to everyone as we go round, if that's OK?'

'That would be fine.'

Ur-r. Now he sounded stuffy and prim. But that was marginally better than what he really wanted to say. Which was along the lines of, Linen cupboard. You. Me. Now.

He'd never, ever done the chest-beating Tarzan-type thing. What was it about this woman that made him feel like that?

'Right. This is Louise, our senior midwife. Known to everyone as Lulu.'

The woman she'd been chatting to. In her late thirties, dark-haired, little and plump with a friendly smile. And a knowing look in her eyes. No doubt a smile from Judith Powell melted the brain of just about every male she met, and it was obvious to everyone that he was no exception. 'Pleased to meet you,' he said.

'And you.'

'Catch you later, Lulu.' Judith took a sheaf of files from the desk. 'Right. Our first mum is Lisa Ford.'

Not 'patient', he noted. Good. So Judith took the modern approach rather than seeing pregnancy as a condition that needed to be treated.

'It's her first baby, she's thirty-four and the baby's breech presentation.'

Meaning that the baby was bottom down rather than head down in the womb. 'So she's in for a section?' he asked.

Judith shook her head. 'She wants a vaginal delivery, if possible.'

'What sort of breech?'

'Frank,' Judith explained. This was the most common type of breech presentation, with the baby's hips flexed and knees extended. 'The ultrasound didn't show anything conclusive but I'd like her to have another ultrasound after delivery—it's possible that she has fibroids in her uterus.'

'How are you planning to manage the delivery?'

'I'm going to try ECV, when we finish the ward round.' ECV, or external cephalic version, was a way of turning the breech baby to a normal presentation, through a kind of forward somersault.

'You're sure she's a suitable candidate?'

'The baby's been breech since twenty-six weeks and I discussed it all with Rowan.'

His predecessor, who'd taken a sideways move to a consultant's post in Birmingham, to be nearer his parents when their first grandchild was born in three months' time.

Clearly Kieran's doubts showed on his face, because she took him through Lisa's case history. 'She's thirty-eight weeks now, it's a singleton baby and not small for dates. Lisa has no uterine scars, no signs of hypertension or preeclampsia—so there's a much smaller risk of placental abruption. Oh, and she's rhesus positive, before you ask. And she's had nothing by mouth since midnight. I've got the portable scanner on standby and the cardiotocograph ready. I thought we could do an ultrasound now to check the position of her placenta and the baby, whether the baby's growth rate is satisfactory and whether the volume of amniotic fluid is normal. Then we'll set the CTG running for half an hour so we can check the baby isn't distressed.'

She was more thorough than he'd expected. Maybe he'd got it wrong and she wasn't a makeweight. Maybe she'd been on her break when she'd been chatting to Louise, not simply wasting time. 'And you're experienced in ECV?' he asked.

'No. But I believe you are. So you can talk me through it.'

He frowned. 'How do you know?' Had his résumé been passed round the ward?

She looked embarrassed. 'When we heard you were joining us from the Hampstead Free, I, um, asked Dad about you.'

'Right.' It was tempting—very tempting—to ask what Professor Powell had said about him. But Kieran had no intention of falling into that trap.

'So will you work through it with me?'

He nodded.

'Great. Thanks.' She flashed him another of those knee-weakening smiles. He didn't dare smile back. The safest place to look was at her hands.

Though even that was dangerous. There was no ring on the left hand, he noted. No white mark either, so it wasn't that she removed a ring for her job. But the lack of a ring didn't mean anything. Tess's ex had never given her a ring, but she'd still been committed to him—and completely devastated when he'd dumped her three weeks ago.

Tess. Tess, who needed him right now. He should be thinking of his baby sister, not lusting after his colleague.

When Judith had introduced Kieran to the patients, written up their notes and introduced him to Margot and Daisy, the other two midwives on duty, they returned to Lisa Ford.

'OK, Lisa,' Judith said warmly. 'The CTG results look fine—the baby's happy. Your pulse and blood pressure are a little bit higher than normal, but I'd guess that's because you're nervous.'

'A bit,' Lisa admitted.

'It's your choice. You don't have to do anything you don't want to do,' Judith reminded her.

Lisa bit her lip. 'Is it going to hurt?'

'It might be a bit uncomfortable, but it shouldn't be painful,' Kieran said.

'I'll be brave, then.' She swallowed. 'Because I really, really don't want a section. I'd do anything to avoid it.'

'We can't guarantee this is going to work—and even if it does, your baby might be one of the stubborn ones who turns himself right back again,' Judith warned gently. 'But that's why we've left trying the manoeuvre until after thirty-seven weeks, to give you a better chance of him *not* turning back again.'

'Let's do it,' Lisa said.

'You might be more comfortable if you empty your bladder first,' Kieran said. 'You'll feel a bit of pressure on your tummy.'

When she'd left the room, he turned to Judith. 'So I'll tell her what you're doing as you do it.'

Judith nodded. 'Fine. I've read up on it—but it's not the same as doing it yourself.'

'If it doesn't work, don't think that you're a failure or that it's your fault,' he said quietly.

Oh, no. Were her insecurities that obvious? She'd had to work hard to get this far. Really hard. Studying a lot longer than anyone else she knew. And if Zoe Hutton, her best friend, hadn't coached her through some of her exams she would have failed.

Sometimes she wondered if she'd done the right thing. If she should have given up and gone for a career in music after all. But she hadn't been able to stand the idea of disappointing her father. He'd wanted a son to follow in his footsteps. Judith was his only child. QED: she'd tried to make him forget that she was a girl, and had followed in his footsteps.

Except she didn't have the natural brilliance of Zoe or the quickness of Holly Jones, her other best friend. She had to rely on reading up on things, and carrying obstetric handbooks in her pockets so she could double-check that she was managing complications properly. She'd only just been made a registrar; whereas Holly and Zoe had been promoted ages before. And Zoe was on the fast track to becoming one of the youngest consultants in the hospital.

A failure? Oh, he could say that again.

Then she made the mistake of looking at him. Lord, he had a beautiful mouth. A full, generous lower lip that made her want to lean forward and touch her own to it. And those dark, dark eyes—so deep she could drown in them.

She only just stopped herself raising a hand to touch his cheek, to find out if his skin was as soft as it looked. Kieran's forebears must have some Mediterranean blood, she thought, because his hair was almost bluish-black and his skin had a faint olive tinge to it. Italian? Spanish?

Before she could make a fool of herself, Lisa returned, to Judith's relief. She helped Lisa onto the bed. 'I'm going to dust your tummy with talc,' she said, 'so I don't pinch your skin.'

'Thank you.'

Kieran took over. 'With her right hand, Judith's going to lift your little one's bottom out of your pelvis. Her left hand's going to be on the top of the baby's head, and she's going to push his head down so it follows his nose—as if he's going to do a forward roll in your tummy. You'll feel her left hand pushing his head down while her right hand pushes his bottom upwards at the same time.'

Judith tried it, then turned her head to mouth at Kieran, 'It's not working.'

'But some babies like to be different,' he said with a reassuring wink. 'They'd rather do a backward roll than a forward roll, so Jude's going to try that one next.'

Judith swallowed hard. It had looked so simple in the textbooks she'd pored over last night. She hadn't bargained for a particularly stubborn baby.

'Take your time, Jude. There's no rush.' Kieran smiled at her, then at Lisa. 'Are you OK there, Lisa?'

'Yes, Dr Bailey.'

'Kieran,' he corrected with a smile. 'OK. Take some nice deep breaths for me. That's it. Relax.'

He had a gorgeous voice. Judith could imagine lying face down on a bed, while his hands eased the knots out of her shoulders. *Deep breaths... Relax...*

She remembered where she was and could have kicked herself. Her mind needed to be on her patient, not her consultant! Even if he was the most attractive man she'd met in years.

'Come on, little one,' she coaxed, almost under her

breath. 'Turn for me. That's it. Keep going. Keep going.' She stared at Kieran. 'Wow. I think he's done it!'

Kieran quickly checked Lisa's abdomen. 'Yep. Well done, both of you.'

'I didn't do anything—I just lay here,' Lisa protested.

'You relaxed and let it happen. That's important,' Kieran said. 'Now I'm going to check your baby's heartbeat with the cardiotocograph again.' He put the sensors back in place and looked at the trace. 'His heart rate's a bit slow, but this happens in around forty per cent of cases—it's all down to compression around the head.'

Bradycardia or a slow heartbeat could also mean that the umbilical cord had been knotted, Judith knew, in which case she'd have to turn the baby back to a breech position and they'd have to admit Lisa for observation—maybe even for a Caesarean.

'I'll keep the CTG going for a bit longer, until I'm happy that the heart rate's come back up again,' Kieran said.

'What happens then?' Lisa asked.

'It's up to you. We can induce you, or you can go home to wait until labour starts naturally.'

'If you wait, there's a chance the baby might turn back again. But if you're induced, there's more chance that you'll need us to help you deliver the baby. So it's your choice,' Judith said.

'If the baby turns again, will I definitely have to have a section?' Lisa asked.

'Not necessarily,' Kieran advised. 'If you'd like to try for a vaginal delivery, and provided the baby isn't distressed, that's fine.' He smiled at her. 'Baby's heart rate is coming back up again, and I'm happy with the trace. Everything seems fine. Do you have any pain anywhere?'

Lisa shook her head.

'Good. If you feel any pain or experience any bleeding,

you need to ring your midwife straight away, or come straight here,' he advised.

'So I can go home now?'

'Rest for a little while first,' he said. 'But as soon as you feel ready to go, provided you're not in any pain, let one of the nurses know and I'll come and check you over before you go.'

'Thank you. Both of you,' she said, looking relieved.

Judith liked his bedside manner, the way he'd made Lisa feel at ease. Kieran Bailey was more than just a pretty face, she thought. And from the look on Lisa's face, she thought so, too.

But as Judith left the room, she noticed a familiar scent. Baby sick. Kieran smelled faintly of baby sick. As she knew for a fact no babies had been sick on him on the ward that morning, it could only mean one thing.

His own baby had been sick on him that morning before work.

And that would explain why he'd been late on his first day.

She sighed inwardly. Just her bad luck. It was the first time she'd been attracted to someone in a long time—and he was married. Or at least involved with someone. The lack of a wedding ring didn't mean anything.

And as for that flash of awareness she'd seen in his eyes, she'd make sure she kept him at arm's length. She had no intention of smashing up someone else's relationship. Hopefully the attraction would fade after a few weeks.

Or even less than that. Memories threatened to choke her.

'Are you taking your lunch-break now, Jude?' Louise asked.

Judith glanced at her watch. 'If that's OK with you, Mr Bai—Kieran?' she corrected herself.

'Fine.'

'Why don't you go, too?' Louise suggested. 'I can bleep you if you're needed.'

Judith remembered her promise to Bella to look after Kieran. Damn. She needed some space right now to get her head straight. But it was his first day. It wasn't fair to abandon him. 'Um, would you like to come to the canteen with me?' she asked. 'I'm meeting a couple of friends, but they won't mind if you join us.'

'Thanks, but…' Something that looked like guilt flickered over his face. 'There are a couple of things I need to do. I'll, um, see you later.'

'Sure.' She wasn't sure if she was more disappointed or relieved that he wasn't joining them. Relieved because she had a chance to put some distance between them. As for the disappointment, it was better this way. Besides, Zoe and Holly would have grilled the poor man until he'd given them his complete life history.

Her best friends were already waiting for her in the canteen. 'Chicken salad wrap, orange juice and the last strawberry yoghurt,' Zoe said, sliding the plates across to Judith's place.

'Angel.' Judith hugged her and sank into her seat. 'You've obviously had a good morning, Holls—you're usually the last one here, not me.'

'So what were you up to?' Holly asked.

'My first ECV, no less.' Judith blew on her nails and polished them on her sleeve. 'Well, with a bit of help from our new consultant.'

'The one who worked with your dad,' Zoe remembered. 'What's he like?'

'OK.'

'Oh,' Zoe said meaningfully.

Judith pulled a face at her. 'Don't take that tone with me—just because you're disgustingly happily married, it doesn't mean everyone else has to be.'

'No.' Zoe flushed. 'Sorry, Jude. No matchmaking attempts, I promise.'

Judith sighed. 'Oh, hell. I'm sorry for snapping, Zo. And you know I'm pleased you and Brad are happy.'

'So tell us about the new boy,' Holly prompted.

Judith took a bite of her chicken salad wrap, making her friends wait. Then she smiled. 'Kieran Bailey? OK. He's taller than me, dark hair, eyes like black velvet.' And a mouth I want to feel on mine. Except I can't have him.

'Are you sure you're not smitten?' asked Holly.

Her face must have given her away. Damn. 'You know my track record with men,' she said lightly. 'I always pick the louses.'

Zoe frowned. 'You said he was OK. What makes you think he's a louse?'

'Because he's married.' Judith fiddled with her glass. 'Why else would he smell of baby sick?'

'Because you work in the maternity unit perhaps?' Holly asked. 'You're jumping to conclusions, Jude.'

'You should have brought him to lunch with you.' Zoe grinned. 'I'd have asked him for you.'

Judith rolled her eyes. 'I know you would, Hurricane Zoe! Anyway, he said he had things to do.'

'Which doesn't have anything to do with being married. You can be single and have things to do,' Holly pointed out.

'Jude, if he's nice and you like him—go for it,' Zoe said.

'You're barely back from honeymoon and you've still got your rosy glasses on,' Judith said, patting her hand. 'It's *so* not going to happen.' Zoe and Holly had been her best friends for years. They knew the score where Judith and men were concerned: it just didn't work. Judith had spent her time at med school studying rather than socialising— gaining a reputation as an ice maiden in the meantime. Which meant the nice men had been scared off, and the only ones who approached her now saw her as a challenge to be conquered and then boasted about.

So nowadays Judith settled for friendship. And as for the awareness that had prickled down her spine when Kieran had shaken her hand…well, she'd just have to learn to ignore it. Because nothing was going to happen between them.

Was it?

CHAPTER TWO

BY FRIDAY, Kieran felt as if he'd been working at London City General all his life. Everyone on the ward was friendly, Bella was the kind of boss who trusted you to get on with your job and see her if you had a problem, and even Tess seemed to be settling a little more at home—at least, she hadn't cried as much as usual that morning before he'd left, and he'd managed to get to work on time ever since Monday.

The only sticking point was Judith Powell.

Because he couldn't get her out of his head. Her smile, her voice, the vanilla scent of her perfume: they filled his senses. The back of his neck started to tingle the moment she walked into a room.

He knew from hearing the midwives teasing her about being married to her job that she was single. Which meant she wasn't really off limits. Except…she was the daughter of his former boss. She was his colleague at work. There was Tess to consider. So, although he was tempted, it would be way, way too complicated if he started seeing Judith—even if *she* wanted to start seeing *him*, which was by no means a definite.

But sometimes when they were having a case conference he caught her eye. And the flicker of a smile that said, maybe. Or was that just his imagination? Was it just that the pull was so strong for him, he wanted it to be the same for her? That same urge to reach out and touch. Taste. Kiss.

'Just the man I wanted to see,' Margot said, breaking into his thoughts. 'You're going to buy a ticket for our fundraiser, aren't you?'

'Fundraiser?'

'Jude's Wednesday night music club.'

He frowned. 'Jude? *Our* Jude?'

Margot nodded. 'Oh, come on. Don't say you haven't heard about Jude's singing. She's...' She stopped, and grinned. 'Well, you can buy a ticket and hear for yourself.'

'Jude sings?' he queried.

'Yes. And we get a third of the profits.'

So who got the other two-thirds? The question must have been written all over his face because Margot added hastily, 'Paeds gets a third and ED gets a third, too. It's a joint fundraiser with them. Jude does it every month.'

'Right.'

'Even if you don't come, you can still buy a ticket. It's for a good cause.'

How could he resist the idea of seeing Judith Powell outside the hospital? 'Sure. When is it?'

'Next Wednesday, at the hospital social club. There's food as well. Zoe Hutton in Paeds makes the best cheese straws in London, and her brownies are to die for.'

Social club. Maybe, just maybe... A lightbulb flicked on in the back of his head. 'Is it limited to just staff?'

'No, you can bring a friend. Or a partner.' Margot gave him a curious look.

Kieran didn't particularly want to explain about Tess— if he did persuade her to come, the last thing she needed was to think that people were gossiping about her. But maybe a night out would do his baby sister good. Teach her that although she'd loved Aidan desperately and he'd let her down in the worst way, there was still a world outside. A world with people who'd be kinder than her ex. His next-door neighbour, Rosemary, would look after Charlie for them—she'd been keeping half an eye on Tess for him while he was at work.

Though if it meant glamming up, Tess would probably

run a mile. He'd have enough of a job persuading her to put on some lipstick. Since Aidan had dumped her, Tess hadn't seen the point in a lot of things. 'How dressy is it?'

'Comfortable. Smart casual,' Margot said.

He might be able to persuade her, then. 'Put me down for two tickets,' he said with a smile.

'So you're bringing your partner?' Margot asked.

He chuckled. 'Honestly. Midwives must be the nosiest bunch going!'

'Well, if you *will* be secretive,' she teased back.

His smile faded. He wasn't secretive. Just protecting his little sister. 'Yeah, well,' he said, and paid up.

Later that morning, Judith rapped on the door of Kieran's office. 'Got a minute?'

'Sure.' More than a minute, where she was concerned. But this was a professional question. It deserved a professional answer. 'What's up?'

'I've just had a mum admitted—Pippa Harrowven. She's thirty-five weeks. She rang her midwife because she wasn't feeling well, and the midwife sent her straight here. I've examined her and I'm not happy. Her temperature's up, her heart rate's up and so is the baby's. She's feeling sick but not actually vomiting, she says it hurts to pee and when I examined her there was some muscle guarding—I think it's more than just cystitis.'

'Has anyone done an MSU?'

A mid-stream urine sample could tell them if Pippa had an infection and what had caused it. 'Yes—I've sent it to the lab for culture and sensitivity tests. Her urine's cloudy, but when Daisy tested it, it wasn't acid, so it's not *E. coli*.'

'Are you thinking acute pyelonephritis?' Kieran asked.

She nodded. 'I was. Except it's not *E. coli*, so that rules it out.'

'Not necessarily. I know *E. coli* accounts for eight-five

per cent of cases, but it could be three or four other organisms, including *Klebsiella* and *Proteus*,' he reminded her. 'Any other symptoms?'

'She's complaining of pain and tenderness around the loins, and it seems to be following the path of the ureters. She said it started last night and it's just got a lot worse.'

Kieran nodded. 'It sounds very like acute pyelonephritis.'

'I've asked Daisy to do her obs, and keep an eye on her temperature and pulse. But if it is pyelonephritis, we're talking possible problems with growth and preterm labour, aren't we?'

'Yes.' Kieran couldn't figure it out. Judith had reached a diagnosis, and from what she'd told him it sounded like the correct one. So why was she still so unsure? She was the daughter of an obstetric professor. She must have grown up hearing obstetric terms bandied about the house—so surely she should be too confident, if anything.

Unless she'd once been overconfident and had made the kind of mistake that made you question every action for a very, very long time afterwards. And Bella had said that Judith didn't want to work with her father. Kieran had worked with Ben for years and found him very fair. There was definitely more here than met the eye, and it intrigued him. 'Want me to come and have a look?'

Her brow smoothed with relief. 'Please.'

'Sure.' He followed her into the ward and Judith introduced him to Pippa.

'I'm just going to examine you, Pippa, if that's all right?' He paused for the young mother-to-be's agreement. 'OK. Tell me if it hurts.' Gently, he palpated her abdomen. As he moved along the path of the ureters, Pippa flinched.

'It hurts. And I need to pee again. Except I probably won't be able to—I couldn't last time, and I haven't had anything to drink since then. And...' She turned her head and a stream of vomit splashed over Kieran's shoes and trousers.

'Oh, no, I'm so sorry,' she said miserably.

'You're not feeling well. There's no need to be sorry.' He nodded to Daisy to fetch a cloth and water, then mopped Pippa's face. 'I've had worse over me.'

'But—'

'But nothing.' He smiled at her. 'We'll have you feeling better soon, though I'm afraid you'll be on bed rest for a while. As soon as the lab results come back, we'll know which antibiotics to give you.'

'But aren't antibiotics dangerous for the baby?'

'We're going to keep a very close eye on you both,' Kieran promised. 'Jude thinks you've got something called pyelonephritis, and I think she's right. It's an infection of the kidney and the tubes that carry urine away from the kidneys, so we'll need to give you antibiotics to stop it. I can also give you something to bring your temperature down, and we'll put you on a drip to make sure you don't get dehydrated.'

'We can give you a heat pad for your back, to help with the pain,' Judith added. 'And Daisy's going to keep an eye on your temperature and your pulse rate.'

'You said bed rest. How long will I be in?'

'A week or so,' Kieran said.

'But I can't be! I—I've got a pile of work to do. I'm a freelance artist. If I don't work, I don't get paid and I'll probably lose my client, and…' Pippa's lower lip trembled.

'Is there someone we can call for you?' Kieran asked. 'And maybe your partner can explain to your client.'

Pippa shook her head. 'He left me when we found out I was pregnant. He doesn't want a baby to complicate things. But I couldn't bring myself to have a termination. And…' She shook her head, choked by tears.

'How about your mum?' Judith asked gently. 'Or a good friend?'

'My mum's in Lincolnshire. I can't drag her all the way up to London.' Pippa wiped her hand across her eyes. 'There's my best friend. Except she's busy and—'

'If my best friend was in hospital, pregnant and ill and scared, I'd be there for her,' Judith cut in. 'It wouldn't matter how busy I was.'

'Sorry, I'm not usually this pathetic,' Pippa said.

'Hey. You're not feeling well, and your hormones are all over the place,' Kieran told her. 'So you're not being pathetic at all.'

'How did I get it?' Pippa asked.

'You're more likely to get it in pregnancy because urine moves more slowly from the kidney to the bladder, due to hormone changes. As your uterus gets bigger, it puts more pressure on your ureters—they're the tubes that connect your kidneys to your bladder. And that means it's easier for germs to grow.'

'So it's not something I did?'

'No,' Kieran reassured her.

'Is the baby going to be all right?'

Judith nodded. 'There's a risk you might go into labour early, but you're thirty-five weeks now, so your baby's got a good chance.'

'But you need to tell us if you feel any tightening around your uterus or stomach cramps or a low ache in your back,' Kieran added. 'We'll test another urine sample forty-eight hours after we start giving you the antibiotics, and you need to have a sample tested every time you see your midwife. It might come back, so you'll need to take antibiotics for about six weeks after you have the baby, and your GP should book you in for a check six weeks after that so we can make sure you're not going to have any more problems.'

'A week.' Pippa shook her head. 'I can't stay in bed for a week. I really can't.'

'Up to you,' Kieran said. 'But if we don't treat you and you end up with sepsis—that's infection in your blood—you'll be here for a lot longer.' If she survived. Not that he was going to frighten her by telling her that now. He'd wait until the infection cleared.

'I'll call your friend,' Judith said. She squeezed Pippa's hand. 'You'll be fine. I promise.'

When the test results came back, Kieran called Judith into his office. 'Well spotted,' he said, passing the results to her.

She read them swiftly. '*Klebsiella.* You were right.'

'No, *you* were right. You said it wasn't *E. coli.* So we can start her on IV antibiotics. I'd like Daisy to do her obs at least four-hourly.'

'Sure. I'll go and see her.'

As she reached the door, Kieran said softly, 'Hey.'

Judith paused and looked round. 'What?'

'Don't doubt yourself. You're doing a great job.'

'I...' Colour washed into her face, and she muttered something he couldn't catch before she left his office.

Stop wishing, Kieran thought. She's not yours, she's not going to be yours. You just work together. Leave it at that.

Except his heart most definitely wasn't listening.

The following Wednesday night, Tess looked dubiously at her brother. 'I've changed my mind. I don't want to leave Charlie.'

'It's only for a couple of hours. He'll be absolutely fine. He likes Rosemary, she used to be a childminder before she retired so she knows everything there is to know about babies, and I'll keep my mobile phone switched on so she can get us if she needs us.'

'I thought you weren't allowed to use mobiles in hospitals?'

'It's in the hospital social club. Different building,' Kieran explained. 'Come on, Tess. It'll be fun.'

The doorbell rang, and he saw the panic in Tess's eyes. He sighed inwardly. 'Look, if you really don't want to come, I understand. But it'd be nice for us to go out and let our hair down. Just for a couple of hours. We don't have to stay late.'

'I won't know anyone.'

'You'll know me.' He wrinkled his nose at her. 'Anyway, it'd be a waste of good lippy if you stay in now.' Lipstick that he'd bought her on the way home from work, hoping it would tempt her into making an effort with her appearance.

'I look a frump.'

She certainly didn't dress as fashionably as she had before Charlie's arrival, but no way could anyone call Tess Bailey a frump. He'd once teased his kid sister that she'd manage to look great in a bin bag. 'Course you don't. And you're going to be on the arm of the best-looking man in the hospital.'

She pursed her lips. 'I thought I was going with you.'

Kieran grinned. That was more like the old Tess—teasing and keeping her big brother in his place. 'You are. Come on, let's get Rosemary settled.'

Tess had an enormous list of things to check, but finally Kieran and Rosemary persuaded her out of the door. And when they got to the hospital social club and Tess froze, Kieran slid his arm round her shoulders. 'You're going to enjoy this,' he said, hugging her. 'And if you're a very, very good girl, I might even let you buy me a pint.'

'Oh, you,' Tess said, but to his relief she let him usher her into the building. They handed over their tickets, Kieran bought them both a drink, and they found a quiet table at the side of the room.

The little room filled, then the hubbub stopped, the lights dimmed and the spotlight lit up the stage.

Kieran's jaw dropped. Judith looked incredible. She was wearing a little black dress and high heels, her hair was loose, she was wearing just enough make-up for him to notice, and his body went straight into caveman mode. His mind followed. All he could think about was rushing onto the stage, yelling 'Mine!' and carrying her off somewhere very private.

And then she started to sing.

Her voice was amazing. Husky and soft. And he felt as if his bones were melting as he listened to her. She looked and sounded like an angel. And he wanted her. Badly.

It was different, tonight, Judith thought. Something was different. She couldn't put her finger on it but…

And then she glanced round the room and saw him.

Out of his suit and white coat, Kieran Bailey was gorgeous. Dark trousers, what looked like a silk shirt—a mixture of purples and blues and greens. All he needed was the earring and a trace of stubble, slightly longer hair, a hat and boots, and he'd be the perfect pirate.

She almost stumbled over the words of the song, despite the fact that she knew it well. Kieran the pirate king. Carrying her off to have his wicked way with her on his ship. Her libido rose and she panicked inwardly. Please, no. She wasn't going to let herself fall for him. She wasn't going to get involved with someone who wasn't free.

Then she saw the woman sitting quietly at the table with him. Holding onto his arm very tightly, as if to advertise to everyone that he was hers. Like Kieran, she had dark hair, but her skin was much fairer. She was pretty, though she looked slightly tired and washed-out. But, then, Kieran had smelled of baby sick. Clearly they had a young baby. And with Kieran working doctors' hours, his wife would be doing most of the childcare, taking the brunt of the broken nights.

Hell, Judith thought. Hell and double hell. He was completely off limits. And she'd just have to stay out of his way until she grew out of this crush, or whatever it was.

The problem was, even knowing what she did, she couldn't take her eyes off him. Which made her the biggest bitch under the sun.

She caught Zoe's gaze and flashed her a look to say, Help!

And Zoe, to her relief, pushed Brad onto the stage. At least singing a duet with her best friend's husband helped to take her mind off Kieran. Though she was intensely aware of those dark, dark eyes. That beautiful mouth. And the fact that he was staring just as hard at her. That he wanted her just as much as she wanted him.

How could he, when he was married—and, even worse, his wife was sitting right next to him? How *could* he?

Whoever the blond guy was, Kieran decided he didn't like him. He definitely didn't like the way the man was singing with Jude. At one point, the man actually put his arm round Jude's shoulders. Way, way, way too familiar. Kieran had to dig his fingernails into his palms to stop himself snarling, 'Take your hands off my woman.'

Because Jude wasn't his woman.

Yet.

'Are you all right?' Tess asked.

Oh, hell. He was supposed to be giving Tess a good evening, not drooling over Jude. 'Fine. Just a bit hungry.' Maybe his blood sugar was a bit low. Maybe that was why he was feeling dizzy—it had nothing to do with being jealous of the blond guy. 'Margot said there was a buffet. Shall we go and get something?'

Tess looked slightly nervous, but nodded.

'Great. Come on.'

But food didn't help. Even with his back to the stage, he was intensely aware of Judith. And he was sure that she was just as aware of him. She'd looked pole-axed when she'd met his eyes—just for a second, and then she'd gone back into professional singer mode and looked as if nothing had happened.

He was going to have to do something about this.

Like asking her out.

Tomorrow.

CHAPTER THREE

'MORNING.' Kieran smiled at Judith.

'Morning.' She didn't return the smile, he noted.

He tried again. 'I didn't realise you were so talented.'

She lifted her chin. 'I beg your pardon?'

'Last night. I was at your fundraiser.' She'd caught his eye. Several times. So she knew he'd been there. 'Your voice is gorgeous.'

'Thank you.'

She still wasn't smiling. Maybe she was just tired from last night. He had no idea what time it had finished because he hadn't been able to stay until the end. Tess had started getting anxious about Charlie and, although Rosemary had reassured her on the phone, Tess had wanted to see her son for herself. No way would Kieran let his sister go home on her own, so he'd left with her. And every step away from Judith had torn at his heart.

'The guy who sang with you—he was good, too.' Kieran hoped he didn't sound as jealous as he felt.

'Brad? Yeah, he's cool.'

'Your boyfriend?' Oh, for goodness' sake! He had no right to quiz her like this. It was none of his business.

He just *wanted* it to be his business.

She frowned. 'Hardly. He's my best friend's husband.'

Good.

When her frown deepened, Kieran had a nasty feeling that he'd just spoken aloud. 'Good that he helps in the fundraiser, I mean.'

'Of course he would. His wife started them, about eighteen months ago.'

From her clipped tone, he was aware that he'd said something very wrong, but what? Hopefully he'd be able to smooth things over during their shift, otherwise, it would be a waste of time asking her out tonight. She'd refuse flatly and it would only make things worse between them. 'I'd better do my rounds.'

'And I'm due at the antenatal clinic.'

'See you later, then.'

Her gaze most definitely said, I'd rather not. But what on earth had he done to upset her?

He was still none the wiser at the end of Judith's clinic, when she knocked on his door. 'Got a moment?'

Still not as warm and friendly as she'd been on the day they'd met, but maybe if he responded as a professional, she might relax with him again. 'Sure. Come and sit down. What's the problem?'

'One of my mums—Rhiannon Morgan. She missed her eight-week dating scan and now she's thirteen weeks. But she says she's had trouble going to the loo. She's getting cramping and abdominal pains which have been getting worse over the last couple of days.'

'Could be a UTI.' Urinary tract infections were very common during pregnancy.

'I wasn't happy about the scan. And she's had some spotting.'

'Threatened miscarriage?'

Judith shook her head. 'I can't put my finger on it, but something's not right. The angles on the screen were…' she waved a hand, as if searching for a word '…odd.'

'Have you done a pelvic exam?'

'No.'

Kieran frowned. 'It could be a retroverted uterus.' He drew a quick sketch to show her. 'You know the uterus is fixed at the cervix but it's partially mobile, and it's more likely to move during pregnancy.'

She nodded.

'Around one in five women have a retroverted uterus—where it's tipped back instead of forward.'

'It's linked with infertility, isn't it?'

'Not necessarily. Sometimes it's associated with endo-metriosis, pelvic adhesions or ovarian tumours.' He tapped his pen on the pad. 'Is this her first baby?'

'Her second,' Judith said.

'It's more common in women who've had a baby before. In pregnancy, the uterus can be tipped back, though it nor-mally returns to its normal position again. If it stays tipped back in the second trimester, there's a risk that the uterus will get trapped—known as incarceration—though it's not that common.' He shrugged. 'About one in three thousand pregnancies, roughly. You'll need to do a pelvic exam and check the ultrasound—retroversion sometimes mimics other problems. If you can rule out a UTI or a threatened miscarriage, it might be a malformation of the uterus.'

'Right.'

Again, that flicker of worry in her eyes. Her instincts had been spot on in the near fortnight he'd been working with her. Why didn't she trust herself?

Maybe he could do something about that. 'OK. If it's a retroverted uterus, what will you expect to find in a pelvic exam?'

Judith concentrated for a moment. 'Her cervix will be positioned well behind the pubic symphysis, there'll be a soft, smooth non-tender mass filling the cul-de-sac, and the uterine fundus will be in a posterior position, behind the sacral promontory.'

He nodded. 'It's pretty unmistakable. What management would you suggest?'

'Give her a catheter for twenty-four hours or so, so we can decompress her bladder, and get her to do intermittent knee-chest exercises—that might put the uterus back into the right position by itself.'

'And if that doesn't work?'

'Manipulation.' She grimaced. 'Though if you use too much force, there's a risk of injury to her cervix, or it might distort the uterus or affect the blood flow from the uterus, so it could damage the baby.'

'Mild to moderate force is fine. She'll be in the knee-chest position and you'll need a long Allis clamp—grasp the posterior lip of the cervix.'

She frowned. 'The anterior lip, surely?'

He raised an eyebrow. Just as he'd expected, she'd picked up his deliberate mistake. 'Exactly. It's not a common procedure, Jude. You really know your stuff.'

Her eyes narrowed. 'So that was a trick question?'

'No. It was an experiment, to prove to you that you know more than you think. Trust yourself, Jude.'

She scowled. 'I'm not a child.'

'I know you're not. What I've seen of your work is good, and your instincts are spot on. But you come across—to *me*, that is, not to the patients—as lacking confidence.' Which was probably why she'd only recently been promoted to registrar.

Her chin came up. 'I'm fine.'

'I know,' he said, as gently as he could. 'Look, if you want to talk to me about anything, I'm very good at keeping things secret.'

Oh, yes. She knew that. Like his *wife*. And his baby. Any other proud father would be showing photographs to the midwives, the doctors and even their new mums. Swapping stories about broken nights and nappies from hell. But Kieran kept his private life so private, anyone would think he was unattached.

Thank God she hadn't done anything stupid. Like asking him to dinner. Like giving in to the temptation to kiss him.

He didn't smell of baby sick today. He smelled clean and fresh. All male, with a citrus tang. A scent she liked. A lot.

This really, really wasn't good.

'I'm fine,' she said stiffly.

He raked a hand through his hair. 'Jude, I don't understand this. Since I started here, we've been getting on well—but today you're snappy with me.'

If he suggested that she had PMT or something, she'd throw her coffee over him.

Then he surprised her. 'If I've said or done something to upset you, I apologise. Just tell me what it is, so I don't do it again.'

You're looking at me, she thought. Looking at me the same way I look at you. Wanting. And knowing I can't touch. 'Nothing,' she said tightly.

'OK. Well, the offer's there. If you want to talk, I'm here. But if it makes you feel any better, Bella has a good opinion of you.'

'Right.' She swallowed. 'Well, thanks for the advice. About the retroversion,' she emphasised.

'Yell if you need a hand.'

Judith nodded, and left his office, feeling sick to her stomach. He was married. *Married.* She'd even seen him with his wife. So why, why, why did she still feel that pull towards him?

Maybe she should apply for a transfer. Not to the Hampstead Free: she wanted to get a job on her own merits, not just because her father was the obstetric director there. Or maybe this pull of attraction between Kieran and her would stop. Please, please, make it stop soon, she begged silently. Before either of us says or does something we'll regret.

When Judith had finished examining Rhiannon and had done a second ultrasound, she was sure that it was uterine retroversion. She explained the condition. 'Did you have anything like this with your last baby?' she asked.

Rhiannon shook her head. 'Not a bit of it. To be honest, because it's my second, I wasn't so worried about getting a dating scan done or anything. But I've felt so weird, this last day or so... My baby's going to be all right, isn't it?'

'I'm pretty sure it'll be fine. But I should warn you, there's a risk of miscarriage if we don't get your uterus back in the right place.'

'How are you going to do that?'

'We're going to try and let gravity help you, first of all,' Judith said. 'So it means you'll be in for a couple of days.'

Rhiannon closed her eyes. 'I was hoping this wouldn't happen.' She sighed. 'I'll just have to ask the childminder to keep Livvy a bit longer for the next couple of days— and nag Greg to get home from work a bit earlier. What if the gravity thing doesn't work?'

'We can manipulate your uterus, very gently. It shouldn't hurt, though it might feel a little bit uncomfortable. I should warn you that again there's a small risk of miscarriage, but it's very, very small.'

'Leave it and I might lose the baby; fix it and I might lose the baby.' Rhiannion sighed. 'Not much choice, is there? I'm in your hands.' She paused. 'Um, is this very common?'

'Not that common. But don't worry, our consultant's very experienced.' And drop-dead gorgeous.

Judith settled Rhiannon into the ward, inserted a catheter and showed Rhiannon how to do the knee-chest positioning which would, with any luck, help her uterus move back to the right position.

Kieran was at lunch by the time Jude had finished—she wasn't sure if she was more relieved or disappointed. It meant she didn't have to face him—didn't have to struggle to ignore that magnetic pull—but it also meant she didn't have the chance to apologise. Because he was right: she had snapped at him. And he hadn't put a foot wrong. He'd found her sore spot all right—the fear she wasn't really good enough to do her job—but he'd encouraged her, not laughed at her or despised her for it.

True, he'd said nothing at all about his wife, but that wasn't any of her business. And he'd been the perfect colleague. Patient with the mums, happy to spend time explaining things to the dads, good-humoured with the staff, approachable if you needed a second opinion.

On a professional level, at least, she owed him an apology. She nipped into the hospital shop, bought him a box of chocolates and had just finished scribbling a note to him when he walked into his office and saw her by his desk.

'Hello,' he said quietly.

Lord, his voice. The slightest trace of a posh accent. It sent ripples of longing down her spine.

But she had to stay in control. 'I was just leaving you this.' She screwed up the note and shoved it in her pocket, then handed him the chocolates. 'To say thanks. You were right about the retroverted uterus.'

'That's very sweet of you, but there's no need. You'd already picked most of it up,' he said.

'Not just that. I wanted to say thanks for the pep talk.' She flushed. 'And, um, sorry for snapping.'

Kieran shrugged. 'No problem. We all have our bad days.'

'Yes.' She should leave. Now. But she couldn't. She was stuck there, watching his mouth. Watching the heat in his eyes. Wishing that things were different. That he was single.

The air felt thick and static—if she reached out, she was sure an electric current would sizzle between them and light up the room.

Then he spoke. 'Jude, are you busy tonight?'

'What?'

'I wondered if you'd like to come out for a drink.'

Was she hearing this right? He was asking her out? 'With you?'

'Yes.'

'*Just* you?' she checked.

He frowned. 'Yes.'

Oh, God. He really *was* asking her out. And if he'd meant it in the platonic sense, he'd have asked some of the others, too. This was one on one. Just the two of them. How she wanted to say yes. But no way could she accept. Not when she knew he was spoken for. 'You must be joking,' she said through gritted teeth.

His frown deepened. 'What?'

'I don't know what kind of women you normally associate with—' apart from his wife '—but I don't do affairs.'

'I wasn't asking for an affair.' Though he was thinking about one right now, Jude was sure. Colour slashed across his cheekbones and his voice sounded slightly slurred. 'I just thought we could have a drink together. Maybe dinner. Get to know each other a bit.'

She folded her arms. 'And how would your wife see that? Forget it!' She looked at him in utter disgust, then walked out of his office, not bothering to slam the door behind her. He wasn't worth it.

Kieran stared after Judith in shock. Wife? What wife? He wasn't married!

Then he remembered Margot's comments. If the midwife had told Jude he'd bought two tickets, maybe Jude had jumped to the conclusion that he was married. But surely she'd seen Tess with him at the fundraiser? OK, Tess had a different father, her skin was paler than his and she'd inherited her father's blue eyes while he'd inherited his father's dark eyes, but surely there was enough of a family resemblance for Judith to have seen it?

Or maybe not. He was about to go after her and explain when the phone rang. By the time he'd sorted out the problem, Jude was nowhere to be seen. He finally caught up with her during her teabreak. Luck was with him, because she was on her own.

'Jude, we need to talk,' he said.

She shook her head. 'I don't think so.'

'I'm not married. The woman you saw me with at your fundraiser—'

'Don't tell me—she's your *sister*?' Jude folded her arms. 'That's what they all say. Sister, best friend—there's always some cover story.'

Kieran stared at her in disbelief. He *was* telling the truth! Tess was his sister. How could Jude possibly think he was the kind of man who'd cheat on his wife? Hell. He'd seen what it had done to his mother when his father had cheated on her. He'd barely started school and he'd had to listen to his mother crying, night after night, when his father was late home. By the time he was six, he'd learned to make scrambled eggs so he could coax some food down her. When his father had finally left her for good, a month or so later, he'd watched his mother collapse in on herself. And it had only been meeting Martyn Bailey that had changed her life. Changed his, too, because at last he'd had a proper father, one who had actually been there to encourage him and teach him things. And, when he was ten, he'd had the kid sister he'd always wanted, too.

Well, he wasn't going to crawl. If Judith could misread him that much, a relationship with her would be a nightmare. One he could well do without. Given time and enough cold showers, he'd be able to snap the attraction between them.

Wouldn't he?

'Suit yourself,' he said coolly, and left the room.

Unfortunately, they still had to work together. The following afternoon, not long after Kieran had signed Lisa Ford's discharge form, Jude came to see him.

'How can I help you, Dr Powell?' He couldn't bring himself to use her first name. And maybe keeping a professional distance would help him keep a personal distance.

Her chin rose. 'As you're the most senior doctor on the unit right now, Mr Bailey, I wondered if you might be able to help one of my mums.'

He inclined his head slightly and waited.

She glowered and folded her arms. 'Rhiannon Morgan. The knee-chest exercises haven't worked. I haven't manipulated a retroverted uterus before.'

He knew what she wanted. And she was going to have to ask. Nicely. This time he wasn't going to jump in and offer. 'And?'

She swallowed. Kieran watched the movement of her throat and had to dig his nails into his palms to remind himself that he didn't want to kiss her there. He didn't want to loosen her hair. He didn't want to kick his door shut and kiss her until neither of them could see straight.

'And,' she said softly, 'I need help.'

'You described the manoeuvre perfectly yesterday.' Before she'd accused him of being a philanderer—and then of being a liar. That still rankled.

'There's a huge difference between reading a textbook and actually doing the procedure.'

'True.'

'Are you going to help me?'

'Help Rhiannon Morgan, you mean.'

She swallowed. 'Look, I...'

Five little letters. Two syllables. She really wasn't going to say the 's' word, was she? Stubborn as hell. And it wasn't Rhiannon's fault. It wasn't fair to let one of the mums on his ward suffer, just because he was still absolutely furious with Judith Powell. 'All right. I'll do it, you assist. What's her blood type?'

'A positive.'

'Good. So we don't need to give her anti-D.' The manipulation was one of the medical procedures which could cause a small exchange of maternal and foetal blood—and if the mum's blood type was rhesus negative and the baby's was rhesus positive, that could spell trouble for the foetus unless the mum was given special antibodies.

'I need a long Allis clamp, and I want the portable ultrasound so I can check the positioning, the baby and the amniotic fluid before and after the procedure. Perhaps you could arrange it while I introduce myself to Rhiannon.'

'Fine.' She paused. 'Thank you.'

He couldn't bring himself to respond with 'Pleasure' or 'That's OK'. Because it wasn't going to be a pleasure, working close to Jude. It was going to be sheer bloody torture—because although his mind knew that she was trouble, his body wasn't listening. He could smell her perfume and it made him want to hold her closer. To bury his face in her hair, her skin. To lose himself in her incredible body.

The procedure was simple enough. Rhiannon was in the knee-chest position, and he grasped the anterior lip of her cervix with the clamp, slid a finger into her vagina and applied pressure to the top of the uterus. While Judith kept up a gentle constant traction to the cervix, following his instructions exactly, he gradually rotated the uterus, sliding the fundus on one side of the sacral promontory.

'OK, we're there. Dr Powell, you can stop now. Rhiannon, you can lower your legs again.' He smiled at the young woman on the bed. 'Well done.'

'That wasn't as bad as I thought it was going to be.'

'Good. It really shouldn't hurt, though you might feel a little bit sore later. Can you lift up your top for me? I just want to put some gel on your tummy and give you another scan—and I'm sure you'd feel happier if you could see your little one moving around.'

Rhiannon nodded. 'Jude told me there was a slight risk of miscarriage. And...'

He squeezed her hand. 'I know. Percentages always seem small until they're personal, don't they?'

He squeezed gel onto her abdomen, then brought the head of the scanner across the gel. 'Here we go. One baby, kicking happily. There's the heart—it's beating nice and strongly. Full bladder.' He did a few quick checks. 'That's absolutely fine, Rhiannon. Your uterus is in the right place and the fluid around the baby is exactly as it should be.'

'Could my uterus slip back again?' she asked.

He shook his head. 'Not now. And you should find that you won't have a problem going to the loo. I want to keep you in overnight, and if anything feels different or you're worried about anything, ask me or one of the midwives.'

'Thank you.'

'That's what I'm here for. Now, I want you to drink plenty. And I'd also advise eating half a dozen dried apricots every day—they're a good source of iron, and they'll also help you avoid constipation.' He switched off the scanner. 'Dr Powell will be looking after you, and I'm sure she'll be able to answer any questions you have.' He nodded at Judith without looking her in the eye. 'Thanks for your help, Dr Powell.'

He didn't wait to hear her reply. If she even made one.

'He's lovely,' Rhiannon said to Judith when Kieran had left the room.

'Mmm.' A two-timing low-life, more like—just like the

last man she'd dated. The man she'd met on a training course, the one who'd claimed that the woman who'd phoned him was a friend.

It had taken Jude three months to find out the truth. That he was married.

And now it was happening all over again with Kieran.

Not that Judith was going to shatter Rhiannon's illusions. As a doctor, Kieran Bailey was fine. As a man, definitely not.

It was just a shame she couldn't get him out of her head.

CHAPTER FOUR

HOLLY finished taping up the dressing. 'OK, Tess. I'm pleased to tell you that Charlie's going to be fine. His arm will feel a bit sore, and he'll need that dressing on for a while to prevent any infection getting in—but at least Kieran's a doctor so he can change it for you.'

'You know my brother?' Tess asked.

'Your *brother*?' Holly gaped. Hadn't Judith said that Kieran was married? And the little boy looked so like him, with fine dark hair and those huge dark eyes. 'I'm sorry. I thought he was…'

'What?' Tess asked suspiciously.

'Your husband,' Holly admitted, embarrassed.

Tess shook her head. 'That'd be funny, if…' She sniffed. 'No, you don't need to know what a mess my life is. Kieran's my big brother. He's letting us stay with him for a while.'

'Right.' Holly coughed. 'Do you want me to ring up to the ward? Or can I ring your mum?'

'Definitely not my mum.' Tess shook her head. 'I'll be fine. I just feel so stupid. I didn't think Charlie could even reach up the stairs. I thought it was safe. He's crawling, but he hasn't started pulling himself up—well, not until today. I put my coffee on the stairs while I was doing my hair, and the next thing I knew…' She scrubbed away a tear. 'I'm such a bad mother.'

'Hey. Of course you're not. Accidents happen.' Holly stroked the little boy's hair. 'You wait till he gets really mobile. He'll be into everything and you'll need locks everywhere, he'll empty your handbag down the loo, and he'll end up falling over and banging himself so he gets a huge bruise about five minutes before you're due to see the health visitor.'

Tess gave her a watery smile. 'Have you got kids of your own?'

Holly flinched inwardly. 'No. But one of my old school-friends is a health visitor and she's got a fund of stories like that.' She forced a smile to her face. 'I'll ring up to Maternity for you. I won't be a minute.'

She escaped to the phone and dialled Judith's extension.

'Maternity, Jude Powell speaking.'

'Hiya. It's Holly. Is Kieran about?'

'Sorry, Holls. He's in Theatre, doing a section.'

'Ah.' Holly paused. 'Well, you'll do. Can you come down to ED?'

'Sure. What have you got for me?'

'Tess Bailey.'

Judith froze. Kieran's wife was in the emergency department? 'What's wrong?' she asked carefully.

'Scald. To Charlie—her little boy, that is. She's in a bit of a state.'

'I'll get someone to page Theatre. Kieran'll want to know if his son's injured.'

'Nephew,' Holly corrected.

'What?' Was she hearing this right?

'You got it wrong, you dope. So all that ranting to me and Zo at Giovanni's the other night... You leapt in completely the opposite direction and hit the wrong conclusion by miles. She's his kid sister.'

'Oh, my God.' So Kieran wasn't married. Tess really was his sister. But she'd been so *sure*.

'Jude, you didn't tell him he was a two-timing, low-life scumbag, did you?'

'Sort of.' He'd told her the truth and she'd called him a

liar. And she'd been formal and even a bit prissy with him for the past week.

'I foresee a very large humble-pie job,' Holly teased. Then her voice sobered. 'Actually, I'm glad he's not here. Tess needs to talk to someone professionally and I'd rather it was you.'

Judith frowned. 'Zo's the paediatric specialist, not me.'

'Charlie's going to be fine. This is a maternity thing. *Post*-maternity. I can't discuss things over the phone.'

Post-maternity? Judith thought fast. 'How old's the little boy?'

'Ten months.'

So the chances were it wasn't a post-partum haemorrhage or severe bleeding after the birth. 'If I said PND, would I be a million miles away?' Postnatal depression was very common, and it wasn't always picked up.

'About two millimetres, I'd say. Good leap this time, Jude.'

'I'm on my way,' Judith said. She called in at the midwives' station on her way out of the department. 'Lulu, if anyone needs me, I'm in ED.' She scribbled a note on the whiteboard. 'When Kieran comes out of Theatre, can you get him to buzz down to me, please?'

'Sure,' the senior midwife said. 'Problem?'

'Nothing major,' Judith said carefully. He hadn't mentioned his sister in the three weeks he'd been working there, so he must have a good reason. And she didn't want him to panic. Holly had sounded very matter-of-fact about Charlie's injury, and she would have told Judith if it had been really serious.

Five minutes later, Holly had introduced Judith to Tess and explained what had happened to Charlie.

'Kieran's in Theatre at the moment, so I'm afraid you've been lumbered with me,' Judith said. 'But you're very welcome to come and wait in his office. I can get you a cup of coffee or something.'

Tess's eyes filled with tears. 'I don't think I'll ever drink coffee again!'

'It wasn't your fault. You didn't know he'd pull himself up for the very first time this morning and grab your cup.' Judith took a touch-and-feel book out of her pocket. 'How about playing with this, little one, while your mummy and I have a chat?' She opened the book. 'Look, here's a fluffy lamb. Can you stroke his coat?'

Charlie's eyes brightened and he rubbed the woolly material.

'It's a real shock when something like that happens, isn't it?' Judith asked, turning back to Tess.

Tess nodded, her face blanching. 'I panicked. My baby was hurt and it was all my fault. All I could remember was that you're supposed to cool a burn, so I put his arm under the tap. He was screaming and screaming, and the ambulance man could hardly hear me when I rang for help.'

'You did the right thing,' Judith reassured her. 'Holly says he'll be fine—because you kept the skin cool, there's a very good chance he's not going to have a mark on him.'

'I was just doing my hair, that was all.'

'Tell me about it,' Judith said with a grimace. 'Why does long hair get so many knots in it? It takes ages to dry, and sometimes I think about having the whole lot cut off.'

'But you've got beautiful hair!' Tess looked at her. 'You're the one who was singing last week, aren't you?'

Judith nodded. 'I saw you with Kieran.' And the way Tess had clung to his arm. She'd thought at the time that Tess was his wife, scared that her husband was going to start seeing someone else. And all the time, she'd been Kieran's sister, not wanting to go out or face people she didn't know. He'd tried to explain and Jude had refused to listen. 'Do you manage to get out much? It must be hard, with a little one.'

'I don't mind. I'd rather stay with Charlie anyway.'

'How about mum-and-baby groups?'

'They're a bit cliquey. I did go, but…' Tess let the idea trail away.

'Might be worth trying a different one. Some of them are vile, but some of them are really nice,' Judith suggested. She glanced at her watch. 'Actually, I'm due a break. I don't know about you, but I'm starving! How about we go to the café, I shout you a cappuccino and a cake, and Charlie can have some juice and enjoy himself in the play area?'

'I…'

'Don't believe the fibs your brother tells you about hospital food. They refurbished our café here, last year, and the food's great.' Judith grinned. 'Which is just as well, because I can't cook for toffee.'

'You can't? But…what about all the food at your fundraiser?'

'Not my work—that's Zoe's. She's my best friend, and Holly's. She does the cooking, I do the singing, and Holls extorts the money. Though maybe we should rope you into selling tickets for us.'

'Me? But I'm—'

'Pretty, with a lovely smile, and you've got an advantage we haven't.' Judith nodded at Charlie. 'Get him to give one of those gorgeous gummy smiles, and they'll be queuing up for tickets!'

Eventually, Judith persuaded Tess to join her in the hospital café. Over coffee, Tess started to relax with her and finally started talking. And Judith's suspicions were confirmed: Tess was definitely suffering from postnatal depression. Though when Tess had explained one or two things, Judith could see why Kieran had missed it.

'You ought to be getting back. I don't want to get you into trouble for being late.'

'I won't be.' Judith smiled at her. 'But it was really nice to meet you, Tess. I hope you're going to come in and show Charlie off to us on the ward. And come out for a pizza with Holly, Zoe and me one night.'

'It's nice of you—' Tess began.

Before she could refuse politely, Judith cut in. 'I'm not being nice. I mean it. You've met Holls, and Zo's lovely.'

'I'm not a doctor.'

'We don't talk shop all the time,' Judith said. 'And you must be used to that anyway, from Kieran.'

'Yeah. He's the best, my brother.'

I'm beginning to realise that, Judith thought.

'I don't know what I'd do without him.'

'Do you want to hang on for him?' Judith asked.

Tess shook her head. 'I ought to be getting back. Charlie needs a sleep.'

'I'll see you soon, then. Do you want me to tell him about Charlie?'

'Would you?' Tess bit her lip. 'I feel so...so stupid.'

'Not stupid. Unlucky. It could have happened to anyone, so don't blame yourself. And of course I'll tell him. Take care.'

Judith kept an eye out for Kieran and when he came back from Theatre, she took him to one side. 'Can I have a word, please?'

'Of course, Dr Powell.'

His voice was clipped and she sighed inwardly. This was going to be worse than she'd feared. But she deserved it. She'd frozen him out for the last week. She just hoped that when she'd explained, he'd understand and forgive her.

'In private.'

He frowned, but nodded and ushered her into his office.

She closed the door behind them. 'First of all, I owe you an apology.'

'What?'

'I've been…less than nice to you for the past week. Since you…' She swallowed. Since he'd asked her out. Since she'd been so desperate to say yes but so convinced that he was married, she'd been rude to him. 'Look, I got the wrong end of the stick.'

'You're not making a lot of sense, Dr Powell.'

If he wanted it straight, he'd get it. And Holly had been right. Judith owed him a very large slice of humble pie. 'All right. I thought you were married. I'm sorry. That's why I flew off the handle when you asked me out.' Not to mention feeling guilty because she'd wanted to say yes. 'And I didn't let you explain—and, OK, I called you a liar and I shouldn't have. I was wrong, I admit it, and I apologise.'

'Apology accepted.'

The words were there, but they weren't accompanied by a smile. But she could hardly blame him for continuing to be cool towards her. What had she thought he'd do—beam at her, tell her all was forgiven and ask her out again? Dream on. She had a lot of fences to mend first.

'Was there anything else, Dr Powell?'

'It's Jude. Please.'

There was the merest flicker of warmth in his eyes. 'Judith.'

OK. She'd compromise. 'There was something else, actually. Tess.'

'What about her?' Suspicion flared into panic on his face. 'Is she all right?'

'Yes and no. She came into the emergency department with Charlie when you were in Theatre. He was scalded but he's going to be absolutely fine.' She filled him in on the details of Charlie's accident.

'Where is she now?'

'She went home. We had a bit of a chat.'

He frowned. 'How do you mean?'

'Just a chat, in the hospital café. Um, Kieran, there isn't an easy way to say this. And I'm probably bending all sorts of ethics here about patient confidentiality, but Tess needs help. I think she's got postnatal depression.'

He shook his head. 'No. It's not PND. I'm not going to betray her confidence, but she's had a bit of a rough time lately.'

'With Aidan. I know. She told me.'

'She told *you*?' His eyes widened.

'Look, I know I've been a cow to you since—well, since I jumped to the wrong conclusion, but I can be nice sometimes.'

He grinned. Just for a second, but he grinned. And then he sobered again, his eyes full of worry. 'She hasn't wanted to go out or shown much interest in anything, but I assumed she was miserable because of…' His face tightened. 'Well. She's told you about him.'

'She told me everything,' Judith said. 'And, before you ask, of course I'll keep it to myself. She said she dropped out of college to be with him and your parents have barely spoken to her since, then she got pregnant because she thought it would make Aidan love her more. And then she found out he was seeing other women. Finally, he dumped her—and you came to her rescue.'

'She's my kid sister. What was I supposed to do—let her move into some damp little bedsit, which was all she could afford?' He shook his head. 'The best place for her would be at home. But she's convinced herself that she's let everyone down and Mum and Martyn won't forgive her—or, if they do, they'll take over the baby because they think she's still a kid and can't cope. Until I can convince her to talk to them, I want her where I can keep an eye on her.'

'Of course you do. Look, Kieran, I was wrong about you and I'm sorry. I couldn't have been more way off beam.' And, after what his sister had gone through, Judith knew that the accusation of two-timing had really rubbed salt in the wound. 'You're a great support to her.'

'But she asked you to tell me about Charlie.' He bit his lip. 'Did she really think I'd go off at the deep end over an accident?'

'No. She's blaming herself, that's all. She adores you, Kieran. She's just seeing things a little differently from how they really are. I think Tess needs professional help.'

He sat down and shook his head. 'PND. Now you've said it, I can see all the symptoms. Everything I blamed on Aidan—it's not that at all. It probably even made things worse between them. And I'm a doctor. How the hell could I have missed it?'

'You weren't the only one. Her health visitor didn't pick it up either. I assume her health visitor knew what was going on with Aidan?'

Kieran spread his hands. 'Your guess is as good as mine. I had no idea there were any problems between Tess and Aidan until she rang me to let me know she was moving. She's always kept things like that close to her chest. I said I'd help her move her stuff, but I had to pull rank before she'd let me. When we got to her new place and I saw the mould on the ceiling, I threw a fit and took her straight back to my place. No way was I going to leave her in that dump.' He frowned. 'But she should have done the Edinburgh questionnaire.' The short questionnaire checked for symptoms of depression in new mums. 'Maybe she slipped through the net.'

'Maybe not. She's bright enough to see where the questions were leading. Maybe she thought Charlie would be taken away from her if she admitted how bad she was feeling. It'd be easy to fake the answers and tell her health visitor what she wanted to hear—that she was feeling absolutely fine.'

'And all the time she wasn't.' He tapped a pen on his desk. 'I still can't believe I missed it.'

'Sometimes it's easier to see things when you're on the outside,' Judith said gently.

'I need to ring her, see how she is.'

'Sure. But don't nag her, will you? She's really upset. It was a genuine accident.'

'You really do have a low opinion of me, don't you?' Hurt blazed in his eyes for a moment, then he pulled the shutters down.

'No.' Judith swallowed. 'Look, I...' There was no easy way to say it, but he deserved an explanation. As much as she could give. 'I'm sorry. I don't have very good judgement where men are concerned. Holls says I ought to have "naïve" tattooed on my forehead. The last bloke I dated, um, turned out to be married. I had no idea. I fell for every single lie, every excuse. Anyway, it means that I get the good guys wrong sometimes, too, as well as the bad ones.'

'Thank you. I think.'

'Could we start again?'

He tipped his head on one side. 'How do you mean?'

'Welcome to the ward, Mr Bailey. I'm Judith Powell, one of the registrars—my friends call me Jude.' She held her hand out.

He paused so long that she thought he was going to reject her. And then his hand clasped hers. A warm, firm handshake. 'Hello, Jude. I'm Kieran.'

He was the one to break the contact. Funny, shaking hands didn't normally make her knees go weak. But she couldn't do anything about it right now. She needed to give him time, time to find out that they could be friends. And time to help Tess. And then maybe—just maybe—they could see where things were heading between them. 'I'll see you later,' she said softly.

'Yes. And thanks for helping my baby sister. For listening.'

He didn't say it, but she could see it in his face. *And for not judging her as harshly as you misjudged me.*

Once he'd reassured himself that Tess really was all right, and wasn't panicking over Charlie, Kieran replaced the receiver and rested his elbows on his desk, propping his chin on his clasped hands.

He hadn't expected this. Hadn't expected Judith to apologise so honestly. And to admit that she had lousy judgement in men. She'd been hurt before, which explained why she was single, not wanting to risk it again—and it might even have something to do with her lack of confidence in herself professionally.

So where did they go from here?

Right now, he didn't have any answers. And she'd been fairly definite about 'friendship'. Anything else was just going to have to stay in his dreams.

Half an hour later, his phone shrilled. 'Must be my day for calling your lot,' Holly said ruefully.

'What's up?' Kieran asked.

'Mum with possible suspected abruption.'

'I'll be right down.' He left his office and saw Jude in the corridor. 'Dr Powell—just the woman I wanted to see. How are you on abruptions?'

'OK.' She grimaced. 'But I'm in the middle of rounds and I've got two potentially complicated deliveries. Can we do the viva later?'

'Not a viva. ED called. But if you've got complications

looming, I'll let you off the hook.' He smiled at her and headed for the emergency department. This was crazy. He was using the feeblest of excuses to make sure he worked with Jude, simply because it was the only way he could be near her.

Not near enough, but he wasn't going to risk another rebuff.

'Can you fill me in on the history?' he asked Holly when he reached ED.

'Erica Somers, aged thirty-eight. It's her first baby, and she's thirty-four weeks. She was in a car crash.'

She didn't say it, but her expression told him the other driver had been at fault.

'She's bleeding, but not as much as I'd expect from her pulse and her blood pressure. She says she hasn't felt the baby move as much since the accident, though that could be worry on her part. Her abdomen's tender, and she's started having contractions.'

'Have you checked the baby's heart?'

Holly nodded. 'Sounded muffled—and bradycardic. I've got a portable scanner coming here any moment, and I've sent off bloods for cross-matching, Us and Es and a co-agulation screen.'

'Brilliant. Have you got a line in?'

'Yep. Large-bore cannula.'

'Superstar.' Kieran gave her the thumbs-up sign. 'Can you get someone to chase up the scanner for me, please? And it might be a good idea to get an anaesthetist on standby, just in case I have to do a section.'

'Sure.'

Kieran went into the cubicle. 'Hello, Erica. I'm Kieran Bailey, the consultant from Maternity. Holly's asked me to come and check you over. How are you feeling?'

'My tummy hurts, but that's OK. I just need to know my baby's all right.'

'Of course you do. We're getting a scanner so I can check things out for you. But first of all, can I ask you a couple of questions?'

She nodded.

'Thanks. When you had your last scan, did they tell you whether your placenta was low-lying?'

'They said everything was OK. I'm having a little boy.'

'And you're thirty-four weeks?'

'It's too soon for the baby to come!'

'He'll be small, yes, but he's got a very good chance if we have to deliver him now. But the scan might show that everything's fine. Would you mind if I examined you while we're waiting for the scanner?'

'No, that's fine.'

A quick examination told him that the contractions were becoming more frequent and the resting tone of her uterus had increased. It was looking more and more like Holly's suspicions were correct. The scan confirmed that it was definitely an abruption. And the cardiotocograph showed that the baby's heart rate was getting slower.

He checked Erica's blood pressure. Not good. 'I'll be back in a second, Erica.' He squeezed her hand. 'I just need to see someone about something.' He hailed the nearest nurse and quietly asked her to confirm the anaesthetist and prep Erica for a general anaesthetic. Then he rang up to Paeds. Zoe answered. He filled her in on the background and asked her to meet him in Theatre.

Then he returned to the cubicle and held Erica's hand. 'Erica, the accident's caused you to have something called an abruption—that means that your placenta's coming away from your uterus and the baby's not getting enough nutrients or oxygen. I need to deliver your baby now,' he told her quietly. 'There isn't time to give your baby corti-costeroids to help his lungs mature, so he'll go straight into Special Care. But the staff here are brilliant and we'll all do our best.' He only hoped it would be good enough. With an abruption, there was a risk of between twenty and forty per cent that the baby wouldn't survive. And the mum was at risk, too, because she was likely to have problems with the blood clotting. 'I'm afraid it means a general anaesthetic.'

'So my husband can't be there? He's on his way in now.'

'I'm sorry. But he can wait outside Theatre for you and we'll make sure he's kept in touch with what's going on.' He squeezed her hand. 'We'll do the best for you, I promise.'

CHAPTER FIVE

BECAUSE Erica's baby was pre-term, rather than using the modern bikini-line incision, Kieran needed to use the old-fashioned vertical incision. The section went without a hitch. But the baby's Apgar score—a rating based on his breathing, heart rate, colour, muscle tone and reaction to stimulation—was worryingly low. 'Three,' Zoe said grimly.

'Keep me posted.' He nodded to the anaesthetist. 'How's she doing?'

'BP's not good.'

'Not good here either.' He worked on the placenta. 'Forty per cent detachment, and I can't stop the bleeding.'

'Syntometrine?' the anaesthetist asked.

'Please.' Kieran kept working to stem the bleeding. If he couldn't, he'd need to do an emergency hysterectomy—meaning that Erica wouldn't be able to have any more children. And if her little boy died…

No. He wasn't going to think that.

Please, just don't let her go into DIC, he prayed. Disseminated intravascular coagulation, or DIC, was a complication where the blood started clotting throughout the circulation, using up the clotting factors so the blood didn't clot properly in the uterus. If that happened, there was a good chance that Erica would bleed to death.

'Come on, come on,' he muttered. 'Zoe, what's the five-minute Apgar?'

'Still three. Resuscitating,' Zoe called back.

'Don't you dare die on me,' he said softly. 'Either of you.' Then he glanced at the anaesthetist. 'We need fresh frozen plasma and platelet concentrates.'

'On their way.'

At ten minutes, the Apgar score was still three. 'Oh, no. He's arrested,' Zoe said in anguish.

'Keep going, team. We're getting there,' Kieran said, hoping that his voice sounded a lot more confident than he felt.

But by the time Erica's bleeding was finally under control, Zoe had made the call on the baby. 'I'm sorry, Kieran.'

'Me, too.' He swallowed hard. 'I'll talk to her husband. Poor woman.'

'Holls said the driver who caused the crash was using his mobile phone while he was driving.'

Despite the fact that it was against the law, plenty of motorists still thought it was OK to drive with one hand and less than half their attention. 'Don't tell me. He got away with hardly a scratch?' Kieran asked.

'Pretty much. He was complaining of whiplash—though Holls set him straight about fraudulent insurance claims, and he hasn't asked for painkillers since. She's also given a statement to the police, who are going to throw the book at him.' Zoe's smile was mirthless. 'And, no, you can't go to the front of the queue to wring his neck. Wait until I've finished.'

Kieran nodded. He hated cases like this. They were rare, but hurt enough to make him question why he'd gone into obstetrics. 'Thanks for trying.'

'I just wish…' She shook her head, grimacing.

'It's not your fault, Zoe. You know the score with abruption. The worse the abruption, the less chance the baby has.'

'I know. It doesn't make it any easier, though.' Zoe sighed. 'Do you want me to stick around when you talk to her husband?'

He shook his head. 'Thanks for the offer, but I'll be OK.' Telling Rod Somers that he'd lost his baby son and had

nearly lost his wife, too, was heartbreaking. Rod reacted
with stunned silence, then shook his head. 'No. No. It can't
be true. I only saw Erica at lunchtime. She was going to
her mum's for the afternoon. Everything was fine then. The
baby was kicking well this morning. I saw his little foot
move across Erica's tummy.'

'I'm sorry. Another motorist hit her car. The crash
caused her placenta to tear away from the wall of her
uterus, and the baby was starved of oxygen. Our paediatri-
cian did everything she could, but the baby's heart just
stopped beating and although she tried, she couldn't bring
him back.' Kieran put a hand on Rod's shoulder. 'I'm so
sorry. The only good news I can give you is that Erica
should be fine. She lost a lot of blood and we needed to
give her a transfusion, but you've still got her.'

'She could have died, too?'

Kieran nodded. 'But we were lucky. She's still here and
she'll recover.' Though he'd asked the midwives to keep a
very close eye on her for the first signs of DIC.

'Could it happen again? Losing the baby like that, I
mean?'

'It's highly, highly unlikely.'

'So she was just at the wrong place at the wrong time.'

'Yes. I'm sorry. I know that isn't enough and it doesn't
even begin to make up for your loss, but I'm truly sorry.
If you'd like to see your little boy, I can take you to see
him.'

'What about Erica?'

'She's still coming round from the anaesthetic, but the
minute that she does I'll make sure you can see her.'

'I just...' Rod sounded dazed. 'I can't take this in. She
only gave up work last week. We haven't even finished
doing the nursery or anything. And now...' His mouth
worked but nothing came out.

'It takes time,' Kieran said gently. 'And we're here

whenever you need to talk. Any questions, I'll do my best to answer them. I'm just so, so sorry.'

'You did your best, mate.'

Yes. But it hadn't been enough.

Kieran stayed with Rod until Erica had come round, helped him break the bad news, then walked quietly back to his office. He rang down to Holly.

'Holls, it's Kieran. Just thought you'd like to know that Erica made it.'

'That's great. How's the baby?'

Kieran took a deep breath. 'He arrested and Zoe couldn't bring him back.'

Holly swore. 'Sorry,' she added.

'You're only saying what I'm thinking. Sorry I couldn't ring you with better news.'

'Not your fault. But I'll pass the information on to the police.'

'Good. Let's hope the bastard doesn't weasel out of it.'

'Times like this, I wish I hadn't taken the Hippocratic oath.' Holly sighed. 'Thanks for letting me know.'

Kieran couldn't face the rest of the ward. He couldn't concentrate on his paperwork either. He'd written the same sentence of his report for the sixth time when there was a knock at his door.

He wanted to snarl 'Go away!' but remembered just in time that he was the senior doctor on the ward, so he was supposed to support the rest of the team. He schooled his voice into neutral. 'Come in.'

Judith walked in and closed the door behind her.

Heaven and hell, in one neat little package. Right now, there was nothing he'd like more than for Judith Powell to kiss him better. But they were feeling their way towards friendship. If he didn't keep himself in check, the whole thing would blow up in his face.

'Zoe just told me about Theatre. Are you OK?' she asked.

'I've had better days.' Understatement of the year.

'Come on. You need a break. I'll shout you a coffee and a chocolate brownie.' She touched his shoulder.

Kieran swallowed hard. 'If I were you, I'd move your hand,' he warned, his voice low.

'Why?'

'Because, after the day I've had, I might do something…rash.'

Judith's voice became husky. 'Such as?'

The temptation was too much. He fell.

He curled his fingers round hers. 'This.' He drew her hand towards his mouth and kissed the inside of her wrist, touching the tip of his tongue to her pulse point. 'And this.'

Judith felt as if her bones were dissolving. She touched his face with her other hand—his skin was soft, with just the beginnings of stubble rasping against her fingertips. She ran her thumb over his lower lip. He opened his mouth and his teeth grazed the pad of her thumb, very lightly. Her body reacted instantly and she swayed towards him, wanting him to kiss her—wanting much, much more.

'Jude. I can't stop thinking about you,' he said, his voice hoarse with longing. 'Ever since I first saw you…I can't take my eyes off you. Can't get you out of my mind. It's driving me crazy.'

'Me, too.' She slid one hand into his hair. It felt good. Clean, silky soft. She moved the tips of her fingers in tiny circles, massaging away his tension. 'But I'm not very good at this sort of thing.' She always, but always picked the wrong man.

'Maybe you just lack confidence.' He gently disentangled her hand from his hair, kissed the palm of her other hand, then stood up. 'Jude, I want you. So much. But we can't do this.'

He was turning her down. He didn't really want her—he was just being kind. She only hoped her misery didn't show on her face. But when she glanced at him, she saw his eyes were filled with tortured longing.

'Why?' she whispered. Why was he turning her down, if he wanted her, too?

'We're colleagues.'

'Doesn't matter. We can be professional, at work.'

He nodded. 'I know. But it's the wrong time.' He raked a hand through his hair.

Did he have any idea how sexily rumpled he looked when he did that? It made her want to grab him and kiss him until they were both dizzy. But the look on his face stopped her. Just.

'My sister needs me right now,' Kieran explained quietly, 'and I can't let her down.'

Judith knew she shouldn't say it. That she should salvage some of her pride. But the words came out anyway. 'You and me…that wouldn't mean letting her down.'

'Wouldn't it?' He swallowed. 'Hell. I want to be with you, Jude. But until Tess is on an even keel again, I don't want to risk making her feel worse. She's not thinking straight. If she knows I'm seeing you, she might decide that she's cramping my style and do something stupid—like moving into another grotty bedsit. If she cuts herself off from me as well as from Mum and Martyn, she'll have no one to turn to. It's not fair to let her struggle on her own. I can't be that selfish.'

He had a point. 'I'll wait,' Judith said softly.

'That's the problem. I don't *want* to wait. I want you right now. And… Oh, hell.' Kieran pulled her into his arms and kissed her.

Judith had been kissed before. Plenty of times. But it had

never been like this. Had never felt as if all the stars had suddenly gone supernova, as if time had stopped and the whole universe had shrunk to a tiny, infinitely bright sphere containing just the two of them.

When he broke the kiss, she was completely disorientated. She had no idea how long it had lasted—seconds, minutes, hours, days? Worse still, she'd untucked his shirt and her palms were pressed flat against the bare skin of his back. She couldn't even remember doing that. But it felt good. He felt good. And she wanted more.

'Um,' she said.

He grinned. 'You sound like I feel.'

'Dazed. Is it me, or did an earthquake just hit the hospital?'

His grin broadened. 'Don't ask me. What day is it?'

'No idea. Though it's got a Y in it.'

'You sure about that?'

'No.' She paused. 'Are you busy after work tomorrow?'

'Tess,' he reminded her gently.

'We could have dinner.' Before he could turn her down, she added quickly, 'We don't have to be long. The Lotus Palace down the road does a running buffet. It'll take half an hour—an hour, tops. We could go straight from work.'

'So if I call Tess and tell her I'll be an hour late...' he began.

'And you make sure you get home when you say you will,' she continued.

'Then she won't worry, and we can snatch some time together,' he finished.

'Enough to keep us going,' Judith said. 'Just you and me. Nobody else needs to know about it.'

He was silent for a long, long time. Just when she thought he was going to refuse, he said softly, 'I thought we were just doing friendship?'

'We were. But…' She took a deep breath. 'It's not enough for me. Not now.'

'Me neither,' he admitted. 'But you said you didn't do affairs.'

'There's a first time for everything.' She bit her lip. 'And if I don't, I think I'm going to spontaneously combust in the middle of the ward.'

'Mmm, and we can't have that, can we?'

He was looking at her mouth. She shook her head. 'Stop it.'

'Stop what?'

'Looking at me like that.'

'Why?'

'Because…' Because she knew he was thinking about kissing her. And because she was tall, their mouths weren't that far apart. Too near, too tempting. She leaned forward and kissed him.

This time, when the kiss broke, he was shuddering. 'I'm going to need a lot of cold showers.'

'Me, too,' Judith said wryly.

He groaned. 'Don't. Now I'm going to think about you in the shower. About being in there with you.'

She could imagine it, too. Water cascading over them. Kieran lifting her. The coolness of the tiles behind her back and the warmth of his body against hers. 'I'm going to leave your office before people start whispering,' she said huskily.

'Jude, they'll whisper more if you go out there right now.'

She frowned. 'Why?'

He rubbed his thumb against her lower lip. 'Because you look as if you've just been kissed.'

Well, she had been. Very thoroughly.

'Your skin's very sensitive, isn't it?'

She shrugged. 'It's a redhead thing.'

'You have beautiful skin. Beautiful hair.' His voice grew slightly rougher. 'I want to see it spread over my pillow.'

'Kieran!'

'Sorry. But I do.' He took a shuddering breath. 'Hell. This is a first. You've turned me into a gibbering Neanderthal.'

She laughed. 'And you were so sophisticated before?'

'Well…' He laughed back. 'More than I am right now. Which isn't saying a lot.'

'Call me tonight.' She took a pen and the pad of sticky notes from his desk and wrote her number across the top.

Kieran watched her. Lord, her hands were beautiful. He wanted to touch them. Wanted them to touch him. Long, slender fingers, short nails filed into perfect ovals, soft, smooth skin. No jewellery. And from somewhere deep inside, he found himself imagining a slender, smooth platinum band encircling her left ring finger.

He'd kissed her. Once, twice. That didn't mean she was going to marry him. So why was he suddenly imagining her dressed in an ivory silk sheath dress, her hair loose, at the altar of a tiny country church, right by his side?

This was scary. Seriously scary. He never, but never got involved this deeply. Or this quickly. It wasn't a good idea to get carried away like this. He should back off right now. Before he did something stupid. Before both of them got hurt.

Then he became aware that Judith was looking at him.

'Sorry. I missed what you said.' Not that he was going to admit what he'd been thinking about. Jude Bailey. Dr Judith Bailey. Yes, it had a good ring to it. But it was much, much too soon to start thinking about anything like that.

'Call me. Tonight. Doesn't matter how late.'

'I'll call you,' he promised.

She kissed the tips of her fingers and blew him a kiss. 'I daren't do a real one. Touching.'

He knew exactly what she meant. 'I wouldn't be able to let you leave.'

'Call me,' she mouthed, and left his office.

Kieran forgot the rest of his report. After what had just happened, his concentration was shot to pieces. He'd kissed Jude. She'd kissed him back. And she'd made him a proposal.

That she'd be his secret lover.

The thought was heady and sobering at the same time. Heady, because his wildest dreams were about to come true: his inner Neanderthal was going to get the woman he wanted. But sobering, because it was going to stay a secret. Were they storing up more trouble for themselves by doing it this way?

But they had no other choice. Not if they wanted to help Tess get better. His baby sister had a guilt complex a mile wide and he didn't want to make it any worse. And there was only way to be sure she didn't find out about it until she was ready to cope: by keeping his relationship with Jude a secret from the rest of the world, too.

Judith was right. He knew that. He just wished it didn't have to be this way.

When Kieran got home that evening, the house was in a mess. There were toys everywhere. The only food he could smell was baby food that Tess had reheated in the microwave—and she hadn't washed up Charlie's dirty bowl or even the breakfast things. And Tess herself, although she tried to smile, had suspiciously red eyes.

'I'm sorry. I meant to clear up the mess, but—'

'Hey. I hope I'm not that much of an ogre.' He gave her a hug. 'It's OK, Tess. You've had a really rough day and in your shoes I'd have spent the whole day cuddling Charlie and to hell with the housework.'

'Really?'

'Really. Come on, I'll cook dinner for us, and you can open a bottle of wine.'

Tess's bottom lip wobbled. 'I'm just hopeless.'

'No, you're not. It's tough, coping with a little one. You've been through a lot lately—not just Charlie's accident, but everything else as well. You've been feeling awful and trying to be brave and hide it from everyone.'

She shook her head. 'No, I'm just hopeless. Aidan was right about me.'

'Let's agree to disagree on that one. Believe me, the only reason I haven't put him straight about his behaviour—or spread him a millimetre thick across the whole of London—is because you asked me not to.' Kieran stroked her hair. 'Maybe if you had a chat with someone about how you're feeling, Tessikins?'

Even her old childhood nickname didn't touch her. She shrugged him off. 'I'm all right.'

He sighed inwardly. Tess needed to see someone, but she also needed to feel it was her idea. If she thought he was pushing her too hard, she might cut herself off from him—and then she'd be completely on her own. He couldn't risk that. 'OK, sis. I'm starving. You open the wine, I'll do the pasta.'

By the end of the evening, Kieran was still no nearer to persuading Tess to talk to a doctor. Maybe, he thought, I should have a word with her GP myself. Tell him what Jude and I think. Ask him how we can get Tess to talk to him—maybe use Charlie's arm as an excuse.

Or maybe Jude would have some ideas.

Jude. He'd promised to call her. He'd put the sticky note with her number in his wallet.

Except it wasn't there. He emptied his wallet and went through the contents twice. Still no note.

Hell. Had he left it on his desk? Surely not.

He grabbed the telephone directory. Please, please, let

her be there. But then he saw the list of J. Powells in the area. He had a one in seven chance of picking the right one, he calculated, assuming that she wasn't ex-directory. But at this time of night, the other six J. Powells wouldn't appreciate a call.

No. This couldn't be happening. Maybe he'd put her number somewhere else. His pockets? No. His coat? No. Hell, hell, hell. Why hadn't he transferred her number to his mobile phone as soon as he'd left the hospital?

Then he saw his briefcase. It was a long shot, but... He emptied it over the dining-room table and went through file after file. And at last he saw the sticky note on the back of one of the files. He grinned, stuffed the files back in his briefcase, then grabbed his mobile phone.

Her answering-machine clicked in.

Doesn't matter how late, she'd said. Maybe she hadn't meant it.

But halfway through the message, she picked up the phone. 'Hello?' she said sleepily.

'Did I wake you?'

'No. Just dozing. I, um, wasn't sure if you'd ring.'

'If I'd had to walk across burning coals first, it wouldn't have stopped me calling you,' he said fiercely, his voice low.

'Good.'

He could almost hear the smile in her voice. 'So, you and me. My secret lover.' He paused. 'I don't want you to be a secret. I'm not ashamed of you.'

'I know. It's just...circumstances.'

'It's not a hole-in-a-corner thing.'

'Kieran, stop stressing. It was my suggestion, if you remember.'

'Mmm. Call me paranoid.'

'No. Just sweet.'

'Sweet?' He chuckled. 'I don't do funfairs and winning teddies for my girl, you know.'

'You mean, you're a lousy shot on a coconut shy?' she teased back.

'OK, I admit it. But I can do other things. We could go punting. How do you fancy a lazy Sunday afternoon on the River Cam, followed by a picnic under a willow tree?'

There was a pause, then Judith squeaked. 'Are you telling me you went to *Cambridge*?'

'Um, yes.'

'So I've found myself a brainy guy. I should have guessed. You're very young to be a consultant, and Dad said you'd go far.' She sighed. 'I'm not academic.'

'You're a qualified obstetrician, Jude. So don't tell me you're not clever.'

'I'm not Cambridge standard. Not *your* standard.'

'Hey. I was always picked last in school teams. I was the one who missed the football pass, or dropped the baton in the relay race, or didn't make the dead-cert cricket catches.'

'I can't cook,' she fenced.

'And I can't sing,' he retorted. 'But between us...' He paused. 'I think we're going to make a good team.'

'Yes.' Her voice grew slightly deeper. 'I know something else you're good at.'

'Oh?'

'Kissing.'

He groaned. 'Jude, this conversation isn't any good for my blood pressure.'

'Or mine,' she admitted wryly. 'I wish I could wind time forward. Until the end of our shift tomorrow.'

'Dinner. Can I hold your hand under the table?'

'Mmm. And we can share a plate.'

'Share chopsticks,' he offered.

'Sounds good.' She sighed. 'I wish you were here.'

'So do I.' He switched to his best Humphrey Bogart voice. 'We'll always have the Lotus Palace.'

She chuckled. 'Yes.'

Hell, this even felt like *Casablanca*. But he didn't think he'd be selfless enough to let Jude go on that plane at the end. 'We'll have Paris, one day. We'll walk hand in hand in the moonlight by the Seine. Go to Montmartre. And I'll kiss you at the top of the Eiffel Tower.'

'I'll hold you to that.'

Good. Because he meant it. He wanted to do all the romantic things with her. Show her off to the world, let everyone know that Judith Powell was his girl. 'It's late. I'd better let you go.' He sighed. 'I wish I could kiss you goodnight properly.'

'You can, tomorrow night.'

'I'll hold you to that,' he quoted back at her. 'Jude— before you go, will you sing me something to help me sleep?'

'Sure.' She sang the first verse of 'Count Your Blessings (Instead Of Sheep)'.

'*High Society.*' Kieran gave a wry chuckle. 'Though I think you're more beautiful than Grace Kelly.'

'Charmer. But I was teasing.' There was a slight pause, and then she crooned 'Summertime' down the phone to him. The song suited her husky voice, and Kieran was enthralled.

'You're amazing,' he whispered when she'd finished. 'I'll see you tomorrow.'

'Tomorrow,' she said.

Kieran pressed the 'end' button. 'And I think, Judith Powell, I'm more than halfway to falling in love with you,' he said quietly.

CHAPTER SIX

SOMEHOW, the next morning, Judith and Kieran managed to act completely normally with each other. No special smiles, no unnecessary touching, no in-jokes to make any of the others on the ward wonder if something was going on between them.

And then Margot took a phone call. 'Jude, you're not going to like this,' the midwife said when she replaced the receiver. 'That was Lisa Ford—she's having contractions every five minutes, so she's on her way in.'

'That's good, isn't it?' Then Judith had a nasty thought. 'Oh, no. Her last antenatal check was with her community midwife, not here. Did she say anything about the baby's position?'

'Yep. That's the bit you're not going to like. The community midwife thinks the baby's gone breech again. And Lisa's insistent that she wants to avoid a section.'

'That means an assisted delivery, then,' Judith said. Before she and Kieran had done the ECV, she'd checked her textbook. Vaginal delivery of a breech baby was possible, but it meant maneuvering the baby to help Lisa deliver the baby's body, arms and head. There was a risk of the cord prolapsing, meaning that the baby's oxygen supply would be cut off, or of the baby's head being trapped. 'OK. Call me when she's in.' And in the meantime Judith intended to double-check her textbook.

'Are you OK?' Kieran asked, a few minutes later, when he saw Judith studying a book.

'Mmm. Lisa Ford's coming in. The ECV didn't work after all.'

72

'You'll be fine with a breech delivery. Remind her that she mustn't push until she's fully dilated, or the baby's head might get trapped. Get her into the lithotomy position, unless she'd rather deliver upright. Put a catheter in, give her a pudendal block if she doesn't want an epidural, and when the baby's out to the umbilicus, pull a loop of the cord down so there's no traction on it.'

'Manipulation can make the cord vessels go into spasm,' Judith said.

'Remember that's "can", not "will". You'll be fine. The baby's weight and the contractions will bring the baby's shoulders down onto the pelvic floor. You'll need a towel round the baby's hips.'

'To keep him warm and improve your grip on the skin as you manipulate his shoulders.'

He nodded. 'Exactly. Press on the baby's inner elbow to get his arm out, then turn him a hundred and eighty degrees to do the other arm.'

'Then back ninety degrees so his chin's posterior. If the head isn't extended, use forceps and the Burns Marshall method, so his neck doesn't bend backwards and fracture,' Judith said.

He smiled. 'See—you know exactly what you're doing.'

'I hate breech births,' Judith muttered. The vaginal delivery of breech births was supposedly becoming a lost art. But not today. Today, she was going to have to face doing a procedure that carried a lot of risks.

'You'll be fine,' Kieran reassured her. 'If you're worried about anything, just give me a yell. But I know you can do it, Jude.'

'I don't want Lisa thinking I've got reservations and then worrying herself into a state. So I'd better get my act together.' She took a deep breath.

'Big smile,' Kieran instructed.

'I don't feel like smiling.'

Kieran glanced round. Nobody was in sight. He bent down and kissed her swiftly on the mouth.

'Kieran!' She stared at him, shocked. They were supposed to be keeping things secret—but he'd just kissed her. In the middle of the ward. Where anyone could have seen them.

'Just trying to take your mind off your worries.' He gave her a wicked grin. 'I would say more, but I don't want your mind going completely off your job, Dr Powell.'

Judith pulled a face at him.

'See you later. And remember that *I* believe in you, Jude,' he added softly.

Judith didn't have much more time to remain nervous, because Lisa Ford came onto the ward. Judith explained the options, and Lisa chose to deliver in an upright position. To Judith's relief, everything went exactly as she'd discussed with Kieran: an absolute textbook case.

Lisa's husband, Stuart, cut the cord, and then Judith handed the wrapped baby to Lisa for a quick cuddle before the delivery of the placenta.

Lisa gave the baby a cuddle, then unwrapped the blanket.

'It's a boy,' she said, her eyes misting over. 'My little Stuart.' She smiled at Judith. 'And we'd like to call him after you, too, if you don't mind. Stuart Jude.'

Judith felt tears pricking the inside of her eyelids. 'That's lovely. I think it's the first time anyone's named a baby after me.'

She called Zoe to come and check little Stuart, knowing that there was a bigger risk of certain birth injuries in breech babies. The collar-bone, elbow and femur could fracture, and the hip and shoulder could become dislocated. Then there was the risk of Erb's palsy, a ruptured liver or spleen or even damage to the spinal cord.

'He's perfect,' Zoe pronounced, and Judith almost fainted with relief.

Lisa needed a couple of stitches, but was otherwise fine. And Stuart wandered round the ward, showing off his baby and telling everyone how wonderful Judith was.

'Told you so,' Kieran said at the end of their shift. 'You did everything right. Just as I said you would.'

'Mmm.'

'So. The Lotus Palace.'

'And chopsticks.'

'I hope your dress isn't dry-clean only,' he said with a grin. 'Because you might get a teensy bit messy.'

'I'll risk it.'

If anyone spotted them, they'd agreed on their cover story: they were discussing breech births and Kieran had missed his lunch. Judith felt a surge of disappointment that he wasn't going to hold her hand all the way to the restaurant, but forced it back. This was their secret. Which meant being sensible.

'Did you ring Tess?' she said when they'd piled their plates from the buffet and sat down.

He nodded. 'Which means I need to leave in fifty-five minutes precisely.'

'Fair enough.'

'It doesn't feel very fair. Not to you.' He sighed. 'I've been thinking about it all day, actually. I feel bad that I'm not able to offer you what you deserve.'

'Don't. I'm happy to settle for whatever you can give.' She curled her fingers round his. 'For the next fifty-four minutes, you're all mine.'

'Absolutely.' Kieran selected a tiger prawn. 'Open wide.'

'Mmm. That was good,' she said, and selected a piece of bang-bang chicken for him.

'I love Chinese food,' Kieran said.

They continued feeding each other choice morsels.

'I feel like a teenager,' Judith said with a smile, when they'd finished.

'Me, too. It's frustrating, but kind of fun.' He slid his arm round her. 'It means I get to spend time with the most beautiful woman in the hospital—the one who can sing like an angel *and* is a damn good doctor to boot.'

'Not that good. Not like Zo or Holls—or you. I have to work at it.'

'It doesn't show to our mums, and that's the most important thing,' he reminded her. 'Anyway, you're the one who spotted that Tess had PND and got her to talk to you. I didn't.'

'Holls pointed me in the right direction. Anyway, when you're as close to the situation as you are, you're not in a position to see what's really happening. So don't blame yourself.'

'No.' He shifted so she was closer. 'I loved it when you sang to me, last night. Did you ever think about turning professional?'

She nodded. 'But if I had, I couldn't have been a doctor as well.'

'So what made you choose medicine?'

'I wanted to please Dad.'

He frowned. 'I know people are sometimes different at home from how they are at work, but the Prof was always really approachable. I can't imagine him putting pressure on you to do something you didn't really want to.'

'He didn't. At least, not intentionally.' Judith wrinkled her nose. 'You see, I'm an only child. Dad always wanted a son to follow in his footsteps. I overheard him once, when I was about fourteen. He was talking to a neighbour—he said he was really proud of what I could do as a musician, but in a way he wished I hadn't been so good, because then I might have chosen medicine and gone on to join him.'

'And that's why you became an obstetrician?'

She nodded. 'Music, for me, is like breathing. It's what I do—it's part of me. But medicine… I had to work at it. I mean *really* work. I even got a reputation for being an ice-maiden, at med school, because I never went out with anyone.'

'Because you were always studying?'

'And, even so, I nearly failed one set of exams. Zoe coached me through them. She dragged me down to her aunt's cottage in Norfolk in the middle of winter, made me a picnic on the beach and made me think about what I really wanted to do—whether I wanted to follow one half of my heart and concentrate on my music, or follow the other half and make my dad happy. And me, too—I'm not doing this just for him,' she added quickly. 'I really like my job. I just have to work at it, whereas music comes naturally.'

'So you chose medicine?'

She nodded. 'Zoe got me to study with her. She said it helped her, that she needed the discipline to stop her skimping on her work. It wasn't until Finals when she got the highest score in the university's history that I realised she hadn't needed any help at all—she did it just to help me.'

'Sounds as if she's a good friend.'

'She is—she and Holls are the best. Holls can be a bit scary, but she's got a good heart.'

Kieran kissed the tip of her nose. 'So have you. And I don't think your dad wanted a son. I think he's pretty pleased with his rather talented daughter.'

'I hope so.' Judith shrugged. 'But after all that, I decided against working at the Hampstead Free with him. I knew I wasn't as good as some of the other candidates, and I didn't want people saying I'd only got the job because of my dad.'

'As soon as they worked with you, they'd know it wasn't true. Bella thinks a lot of you. And I'm pleased you're on my team.' He nuzzled her cheek. 'Have a little faith in yourself, Jude. You're a good doctor.'

She shifted uncomfortably. She wasn't fishing for compliments and she didn't want Kieran to think that she was clingy and needy. Just, sometimes, she wasn't sure she'd made the right choice. She decided to change the subject. 'So what made you choose obstetrics?' she asked.

'I knew when I was little that I wanted to be a doctor. And when Mum was pregnant with Tess, I was fascinated by her bump and the way the baby kicked when I tickled the bump. I did think seriously about going into emergency medicine, but I like the continuity of care in maternity—the way you see mums right from the first scan up to taking their newborn home.'

'Clever *and* a softie,' she teased. She turned her face to kiss him, and Kieran groaned.

'My self-control is getting way too much exercise. All I want to do right now is pick you up, throw you over my shoulder and haul you back to my cave.'

'And then what?'

He raised an eyebrow. 'What do you think?'

'Considering you look like a pirate…'

'A what?'

'Like a Spanish corsair.'

He grinned. 'Kieran's a Gaelic name, not Spanish.'

'Well. You look a bit Mediterranean. Tall, dark, dark-eyed, and…' She pursed her lips.

'And?' he prompted.

'Have dinner with me tomorrow night,' she promised huskily, 'and I'll tell you the rest.'

'Dinner? I'm intrigued. You said you can't cook.'

She laughed. 'I can't. But I *can* buy finger food from the supermarket.'

Kieran traced the line of her jaw with his forefinger.

'You could feed me burned toast, Jude, and I really wouldn't care.'

'I was thinking more along the lines of smoked salmon parcels, canapés and strawberries.'

'Then I'll bring champagne,' Kieran said. 'I'm on a late. Is that OK?'

'Very OK. I'm on an early. So that means I get time to tidy my house.' She scribbled directions on a napkin and talked him through them. 'Got it?'

'I'll call you if I get lost.' He glanced at his watch. 'I want to stay—but I have to go.'

'I understand.'

He kissed her lightly. 'Do I have time to walk you home first?'

'No, but that's fine. It's broad daylight out there.'

'Even so, I'd be happier if you took a taxi. I can sort one out while I settle the bill.'

'We're going halves.'

'You're providing dinner tomorrow,' he pointed out, 'so tonight's my turn.'

She couldn't argue with that.

'See you tomorrow.' He stroked her cheek, smiled and stood up.

Judith watched him leave. Noticed how many female heads turned to watch him leave, too. Tough, she thought. He's spoken for. Mine.

She still couldn't believe how quickly she'd clicked with Kieran. How easy it was to talk to him. She'd told him things she'd never told anyone else before. So either this was the real thing, or she was making the biggest mistake of her life.

Knowing her judgement where men were concerned, it was the latter. But Kieran was different…wasn't he?

* * *

Judith hardly got a chance to say more than hello to Kieran, the next day—her shift was busy, and he was with a patient when she left. She dashed to the supermarket and selected her favourite foods—things she hoped he'd like too—then tidied the house. She just had time to have a quick shower and change. On impulse, she chose the black dress she'd worn at the concert, left her hair loose and added the lightest coat of lipstick. She'd just put some soft classical music on the stereo and lit half a dozen vanilla-scented candles in her living room when the doorbell rang.

'Hi.'

In a dark suit, white shirt and sober silk tie, Kieran looked positively edible. Judith was glad she'd dressed up rather than going for something comfortable but scruffy.

'Hi, yourself. Come in.'

'For you.' He handed her an enormous bouquet of roses.

'Thank you. They're gorgeous.' She buried her face in the flowers and inhaled their sweet scent. 'Wherever did you get them at this time of night?' she asked.

He tapped his nose. 'Trade secret. This is also for you. Well, for us.' He gave her a carrier bag.

She glanced inside. Champagne—it was chilled, too. 'Oh, yes!' she said in delight as she spied a box of her favourite chocolates. 'Thanks.'

'I've booked a taxi to pick me up, so I get more time with you.' He glanced at his watch. 'Fifty-nine minutes and counting.'

'Come and sit down. And feel free to lose the jacket and tie.' She ushered him into the living room. 'I take it that you're not planning to drive at all tonight?'

'No.'

'Then you can open this while I get the glasses.' She handed him the bottle.

When she returned, bearing two glasses and the first plate of canapés, Kieran had removed his jacket and tie. He'd undone the top button of his shirt, exposing his throat, and Judith itched to forget the canapés and taste his skin instead.

But that wasn't what tonight was about.

Small steps, she reminded herself. Small steps.

Kieran uncorked the champagne without spilling a drop. He filled their glasses, handed one to her, then clinked his own against it. 'To us,' he said softly.

'To us.' She echoed the toast, and sipped her champagne. 'Mmm. This is gorgeous. But very decadent.'

'And smoked salmon canapés by candlelight aren't?' he teased.

'Well.' She wrinkled her nose at him, and offered him a smoked salmon parcel filled with smoked salmon pâté.

'Very nice.' He took another, and rubbed it gently along her lower lip. 'Open your mouth, Jude,' he said huskily.

His eyes were very, very dark. You want me as much as I want you, Judith thought. The question is, which one of us is going to crack first?

The smoked salmon was followed by tiny water biscuits topped with Brie and black grapes, and then by chicken satay with peanut dipping sauce.

But the strawberries and white chocolate mousse proved Kieran's undoing. He dipped a strawberry into the mousse, fed it to Judith and then kissed her.

The rest of the fruit was forgotten as Jude kissed him back. The next thing she knew, he was stretched out on the sofa, his shirt was completely undone, and she was lying on top of him. His hand was resting on the nape of her neck, under her hair, and his fingers were millimetres away from the top of her zip.

'What happened to taking things slowly?' he asked, his eyes crinkling at the corners. But when she tried to pull away, embarrassed, she became aware that his other hand was at the base of her spine—and the pressure on her back told her that he had no intention of letting her move away.

'You tell me. You were there as well,' she challenged.

'Your hair's so soft. So heavy. So beautiful. The candle-light's given you a halo. A kind of *Beata Beatrix* look.'

'A what?'

'It's a painting by Rossetti. Of the second most beautiful redhead in the world.' His eyes glittered, challenging her to ask who the first one was.

Judith retaliated by switching the subject. 'Did you shave when you went off duty?'

'Yes.' He rubbed the pad of his thumb just under her lower lip. 'And, yes, it was because of you. I didn't want to mark your skin again.'

'You feel good.' She stroked his face. 'I've wanted to do that since the minute I first saw you.'

'I saw you first. Sitting on a desk, swinging those gorgeous long legs and gossiping to the midwives.'

'I was *not* gossiping.'

His expression said very clearly, Oh, yes, you were. 'Then you laughed. You tipped your head back. And I wanted to do...*this*.' He rolled so that she was lying beneath him, her chin tipped up and her throat exposed, and he drew a necklace of kisses around her throat.

'Keep that up, and you're going to be very, very late home,' Judith warned huskily. 'Because I'm not going to be able to let you walk out of here.' She wrapped her legs round him.

It was his turn to gasp. 'Jude. I don't want to walk out of here. You know that. But I have to.'

'I wish you didn't.' She slid her fingers into his hair. 'Mmm. Definitely a pirate king. I can just see you with slightly longer hair and an earring.'

'Captain Hook?' He nibbled at her lower lip.

'A bad boy. And I'd redeem you.'

He grinned. 'No, Jude. You'd tempt me to show you just how bad I could be. You, me, a treasure island... Mmm. I'd take you back to my treasure cave. Take off your clothes. Adorn you in diamonds and pearls.'

'And have your wicked way with me under the stars?'

'Mmm. Starting right here.' Just as he bent his head again, there was a loud hooting outside.

'Hell, no. It can't be.' He glanced at his watch and grimaced. 'Someone's been fiddling with time, put it on fast forward. It can't be that late.'

The hooter sounded again.

He kissed her swiftly, climbed off the sofa and restored order to his clothes. 'We have to do something about this, Jude. This isn't good for my blood pressure.'

'Or mine. When's your next day off?'

'Monday week.'

She regarded him thoughtfully. 'If I change my off duty, we could spend the day together.'

Kieran shrugged his jacket on. 'How? I can't tell Tess about us yet. I still haven't persuaded her to see the doctor.'

'An hour's not enough,' she said softly. 'There must be some way round it. Some way that we can snatch a day.' Right now, a night was out of the question. She knew that. But surely a day was do-able?

'Maybe I can tell her I'm on a course—she won't be able to ring me direct, but I'll leave my mobile switched on so she can text me if she needs me.'

She drew his fingers to her mouth and kissed them. 'I won't ask you to lie to your sister for me.'

'Maybe if I say I need to be somewhere on Monday and it's work-related. That's just...a little distortion of the truth. I need to be with you—and I work with you, so that's work-related.' He pulled her close. 'I'll think of something. Somehow. To get us some time without hurting Tess.'

The taxi horn blasted again.

Kieran tore himself away reluctantly. 'I'll see you tomorrow.'

'Tomorrow,' she repeated.

At work. As colleagues, maybe even friends.

But it wasn't going to be anywhere near enough.

CHAPTER SEVEN

KIERAN was on a late the next morning and came in to discover a brief email from Judith. *Monday sorted.* If anyone else read the message, they wouldn't have a clue what she was talking about, but Kieran knew exactly what she meant. She'd managed to switch her off-duty day.

Life was looking up.

Until the middle of the afternoon, when Margot buzzed through to him. 'Kieran, we've got a possible emergency section in labour room five. Jude's with Sara—the mum—at the moment. She asked me to get you.'

'On my way,' Kieran said. As soon as he rapped on the door, Judith came out.

'Sara Cox, aged thirty-three, first baby. No complications during the pregnancy or labour—until now. There was a bit of blood when her membranes ruptured a minute or so back.'

'Fresh?'

She nodded. 'And the baby's showing signs of distress—more than I'd expect. I'm thinking vasa praevia.'

Vasa praevia was a medical emergency. A blood vessel from the placenta or umbilical cord crossed the birth canal, and the vessel could tear when the cervix dilated, or it could get compressed between the baby's head and the walls of the birth canal. Either way, the baby could die from blood loss when the vessel ruptured—as few as one in twenty babies survived.

'Margot said she'd bleeped the anaesthetist. If you're right, we'll need to do a section and the baby will need a transfusion. We'll need cross-matched blood and someone

85

from the neonatal team here,' Kieran said. 'You'll do the section with me?'

'Yes, but I haven't come across an actual case before.'

'It's rare—one in three thousand. OK. Let's see what's going on.'

Judith introduced him to Sara and her partner Mick.

'I'm just going to take a look at you and the baby, if I may, Sara.' At her nod, he examined her, checked the traces, then looked at Judith. 'Sara, your baby's showing signs of severe distress and I think it may be a condition called vasa praevia, where a blood vessel is in the wrong place so delivering the baby will be tricky. We may need to give the baby a blood transfusion straight after birth. But we need to deliver your baby right now, so I need your consent for an emergency Caesarean.' A quick glance showed him that Sara hadn't had an epidural, and there wasn't time to arrange a spinal block. 'I'm afraid it'll be under a general anaesthetic, so your partner won't be able to come into Theatre with you. But he can see the baby as soon as possible afterwards.'

'Sara doesn't want a section,' Mick stated.

'It's that, or lose the baby,' Kieran said quietly. 'I'm sorry, we don't have time to argue the point.'

'I don't want to lose my baby. Let's do it,' Sara said.

'But we agreed—' Mick began.

'Can I have a quick word in private, Mr Cox?' Judith asked. At his nod, she took him into the corridor. 'I don't want to say this in front of Sara because I don't want her to panic.' She quickly explained vasa praevia to Mick. 'Sometimes it can be diagnosed before labour, but we can only really do it with a specialist test known as a transvaginal sonography—vasa praevia's very rare so we don't tend to scan for it routinely. But the risks to babies with vasa praevia are very, very high. If we don't give Sara a Caesarean and deliver the baby now, he'll literally bleed to death—very quickly. In cases like Sara's, where we haven't been able to diagnose vasa praevia before labour and deliver the baby by Caesarean section—which is the safest way—ninety-five per cent of the babies die from blood loss.'

'But a Caesarean's a major operation.'

'I know. But without it, your baby won't survive.'

'Might he die even if Sara has the Caesarean?'

'There's a possibility, yes,' Judith said, taking his hand and squeezing it. 'He'll need to be resuscitated and have a blood transfusion after the birth. But if anyone can save your baby, Kieran will.'

'I don't suppose we've got a choice, then,' Mick said bleakly.

'There's always a choice,' Judith said. 'If you're both really against having a section, we won't force it on you. But you need to know all the options and consequences so you can make an informed decision.'

Mick sighed. 'OK. I'm sorry. I was being selfish—thinking that Sara won't be able to do much for weeks after the birth, and I can't get the time off work.'

'A section isn't an easy option,' Judith agreed. 'But we'll give you all the support we can. The health visitor and your community midwife can help after the birth, too.'

Things moved quickly after that. Jan, the consultant from the neonatal team, came into Theatre with Kieran and Judith, Kieran delivered the baby, and Jan took over with the baby while Kieran and Judith stitched Sara up again.

'He's still not breathing and it's been five minutes,' Jan reported. 'I can't get a heartbeat.'

'I've already lost one baby this week. That's one too many,' Kieran said softly.

'Oh, I'm not giving up yet,' Jan said, grim determination in her voice.

'What about the blood loss?' Judith asked.

'About fifty per cent, I'd say. He'll be in NICU for a while.'

They all knew what Jan wasn't saying—*if* she could get the baby back in the first place.

'Mick's probably going frantic out there,' Judith said quietly. 'Do you want me to give him an update?'

'Wait another five minutes,' Kieran advised. 'If you give him an update on how things are now, he'll be worrying even more.'

Then they heard a quiet 'Yes!' from the corner of the room.

'Baby's back. Transfusing now,' Jan reported.

Judith saw Kieran's eyes crinkle—his smile was still hidden by his mask. 'Good work. Thanks, Jan.' He nodded at Judith. 'If you want to go and tell Mick the good news, I'll finish here.'

When Sara was out of Recovery and back on the ward, Baby Cox had been settled into the neonatal intensive care unit and Mick had promised to go and see the baby and bring a photograph back for Sara to see, Kieran and Judith flopped down in the rest lounge.

'I really, really don't want another week like this. One baby I couldn't save, another heading that way…' Kieran groaned and closed his eyes. Then he sat up again and looked at Judith. 'Though I wouldn't have missed the high points of this week for anything.'

'Having my first baby named after me,' Judith said.

A smile flickered at the corner of his mouth. 'I had something else in mind.'

Oh, yes. She knew what he meant all right. Holding hands in the Lotus Palace. Talking to each other late at night on the phone. The kisses they'd shared by candlelight in her living room. 'Pirate king,' she murmured.

'Mmm, that reminds me.' He stood up, walked over to

his locker and extracted an envelope. He threw it over to Judith, who caught it in her right hand.

'And this is…?' she asked.

'Yours. Open it.'

Inside was a tiny Captain Hook on a keychain. Judith grinned. 'My own pirate.'

He leaned back against the lockers. 'As I said, I don't do coconut shies. But pirates… Yes, I can do pirates.'

She remembered their conversation about the treasure cave, and shivered in anticipation. 'Monday,' she said huskily.

'Mmm. Monday.' Again, he gave her a half-smile, and Jude felt her knees go weak. 'I've got plans for Monday.'

Her heart rate speeded up. 'Going to tell me what they are?'

He shook his head. 'It wouldn't be a surprise, then.'

She groaned. 'Monday's too far away.'

'Agreed.' He walked swiftly over to the door, locked it, pulled the blinds, then came to stand in front of Judith. He took her hands and pulled her to her feet. 'So this is on account,' he said softly, and bent his head slightly.

When the doorhandle rattled, they broke the kiss. Judith's hands were still entangled in Kieran's hair, and his palms were flat against her back under her loose shirt.

'Just as well I locked the door,' he murmured wryly. 'Coming,' he called to whoever was on the other side of the door.

Judith restored order to his hair while he straightened her clothes, and she sprawled back in her chair as he unlocked the door. 'We'll have to get Maintenance to look at that lock,' Kieran said cheerfully. 'Must have slipped again.'

'Yes.' Louise, the senior midwife, smiled at him. 'I hear you were a hero this afternoon.'

'Not me, Lulu. It was a team effort,' he said. 'Jan's back in NICU but Jude and I are… Well.' He shrugged. 'We need caffeine but it's just too much effort to go to the canteen and get some. So we flaked out here, in the hope someone would come along and take pity on us.'

'Oh, poor babies,' Louise said with a grin. 'Was that a hint?'

'Was that an offer?' Kieran asked, returning the grin.

She rolled her eyes. 'Honestly. Doctors.'

'He'll be your slave,' Judith promised. 'So will I.'

Louise chuckled. 'All right. What do you want?'

'Lulu, you're an angel. Thank you.' Kieran took a note from his wallet. 'Coffee and a sandwich for me, please—I don't care what sort it is, as long as it's food. Jude?'

'Same for me, too, please.'

'And whatever you want,' Kieran added, smiling at Louise.

'I don't think the canteen can do George Clooney with ribbon round his neck and a note saying "Happy birthday, Lulu",' the midwife teased.

'It's not your birthday until next week,' Judith reminded her.

'I don't mind having an early present,' Lulu retorted, laughing. 'So it's food and coffee for both of you—white, no sugar, isn't it?'

'Yes, please,' Kieran and Judith chorused.

When the midwife left, shutting the door behind her, Kieran dropped into the chair next to Judith and curled his fingers round hers. 'Safe from gossip.'

'This time,' Judith agreed wryly.

'So I'll have to wait until Monday. Talk to me, Jude. Take my mind off it.'

'OK. Lulu's birthday. She's forty next Thursday.'

'Mmm, I signed the card and put money in the envelope yesterday. Daisy said she was getting her some posh earrings, chocolates and a DVD.'

'Yep. And we're going to decorate her office. We can't

get George Clooney for her, but we could do second best.'
She eyed him speculatively.

Kieran lifted his free hand in a halt sign. 'No. Absolutely not. I'm not dressing up as George Clooney.'

'Just to give her a birthday kiss. In scrubs,' Judith wheedled.

'Nope. There's only one woman I want to kiss.' He leaned over and kissed the tip of her nose. 'Uh. I shouldn't have done that. Talk to me, Jude. Stop me kissing you properly.'

Her gaze was fixed firmly on his mouth. The mouth that had traced a necklace of kisses round her throat last night. 'I can't remember what I was saying.'

'Lulu's birthday. George Clooney. Have you thought about making her a life-sized cardboard cut-out?'

'With a ribbon and a tag? Oh, yes!' Judith grinned. 'Brilliant. So you're not just a pretty face.'

'*Pretty?*' Kieran pulled a disgusted face. 'Hardly.'

'I never did get to tell you, did I?'

'What?'

'Last night. The other bit. Tall, dark and… No, I suppose "pretty" doesn't quite work,' she teased.

'If Lulu wasn't due back any minute now with our sandwiches, I'd make you say it properly.'

'Oh, yes?'

He moistened his lower lip. 'I can be very…persuasive.'

'Monday.' Judith brought their joined hands up to her mouth and kissed his fingers before releasing his hand. 'On Monday, I'm open to persuasion.'

By Monday, Kieran was panicking. Supposing Jude changed her mind? Supposing there was a delay on the Tube so she thought he'd stood her up? Supposing…?

But when he walked out of the station at five minutes to ten, he saw her waiting for him where they'd agreed, next to the railings outside the Houses of Parliament. She was wearing a bright pink top that really should have clashed with her hair, but it worked—more than worked. With her hair loose, and dressed in faded denims and flat loafers, Jude looked a million dollars.

He smiled as he reached her. 'Hi.'

'Hi.'

'Um. I'm a bit out of practice at this. Dating. I was going to bring you a single red rose, but I thought it might be a bit naff.'

She smiled back at him. 'Hey. We've got a whole day together. Let's not waste it in worrying.'

'You're right.' He slid one arm round her shoulders. 'Let's go.'

'Where are we going, by the way?' she asked as they headed for the other side of the river.

'Surprise. Well, not *that* much of a surprise,' he admitted. It was hard to miss the biggest observation wheel in Europe—particularly when it was right in front of them.

She followed his gaze. 'You got tickets for the London Eye?'

'I thought it was the next best thing to the Eiffel Tower.'

She slid her arm round his waist and hugged him. 'Wonderful. It's on my list of things I want to do, but I hadn't got round to it yet.'

'On a clear day, like today, you can see for miles,' Kieran told her.

Kieran had pre-booked their tickets so they didn't have to queue for long before they got into their capsule. They sat simply holding hands as their capsule began to rise on the wheel very slowly.

Then Judith realised that the woman next to her was holding a hand to her chest.

'Are you all right?' she asked.

'I don't think so—it hurts. And I feel dizzy,' the woman said. 'I can't breathe.'

'I'm a doctor,' Judith told her.

'I've got pins and needles. Oh, my God. I'm having a heart attack!'

'Not all chest pain means a heart attack,' Judith said gently. It could be angina, indigestion or even a fractured rib. And the woman's hand was flat against her chest, rather than clenched in what was known as a positive Levine sign, often given by those who were having a heart attack. 'What's the pain like?'

'It just hurts,' the woman moaned.

Without Judith having to ask him, Kieran was already crouching in front of the woman and holding her hands. 'Have you had any pains like it before?' he asked.

She shook her head.

'Can you lean forward for me?' he asked gently.

The woman did so.

'Does it feel any different now?' he asked.

She shook her head and straightened up again. 'I can't breathe.'

'Jude, have you got a paper bag?' he asked.

'No. I'll see if I can get one.'

While she asked the other passengers in their capsule, Kieran checked the woman's pulse. 'Tell me more about the pain,' he said. 'Does it feel like someone's doing something to you?'

She shook her head. 'I don't know. I feel strange. Like I'm not here. My mouth's dry.'

'Is the pain moving anywhere?'

'No. It's just here.' She rubbed her chest.

Judith returned with a paper bag.

'What's your name?' Kieran asked the woman.

'Sylvia.'

'All right, Sylvia. I'm going to help you breathe. I'd like

you to put the end of this paper bag over your nose and mouth, then breathe into it.'

She nodded, and started to breathe into the bag. Within a few minutes, her panicked breaths had slowed to normal, and she took the bag away from her face. 'The pain's gone,' she said in surprise.

'I don't think you were having a heart attack,' Kieran said quietly. 'It looked more like a panic attack.'

'Panic? But…' Sylvia frowned. 'I'm OK with heights. I mean, I don't like roller-coasters, but this isn't like that. It's safe. And… Oh, I'm so sorry. I've made such a fool of myself.'

'Not at all. Panic attacks sometimes happen when you're looking forward to something, too—it's an exaggeration of your body's normal response to fear, stress and excitement,' he explained.

'So what does that mean?' Sylvia asked.

'When you're afraid or stressed or excited, your body goes into fight or flight mode—it produces adrenalin, which makes your muscles tense up. Your body also demands more energy, and your muscles need oxygen to help them make sugar into energy, so your breathing gets faster to help your body get more oxygen to make energy.'

'And that's what makes it hurt?' Sylvia asked.

'Sort of. When you're breathing very fast—what we call overbreathing—you breathe out too much carbon dioxide. That changes the acidity of your blood, and that's what causes the palpitations, cramp and pins and needles. The symptoms are frightening, and a vicious circle starts—your body responds to the fear by producing more adrenalin, you breathe even faster, the palpitations and what have you get worse, and your body reacts by producing more adrenalin,' Judith added.

Sylvia nodded. 'So how does breathing into a paper bag help?'

'When you breathe back in again, you're taking in more carbon dioxide and less oxygen. That helps to balance the acidity of your blood, and gradually your breathing will go back to normal. If it happens again and you haven't got a paper bag handy, you can cup your hands over your mouth—it'll do the same sort of thing,' Kieran explained.

'So I'm not going to die?' Sylvia asked.

'No. The chest pain's caused by the panic attack—the messages sent from your brain to various parts of your body go into overdrive and it makes you feel pain. Though it'd be a good idea to have a word with your GP. He might run some tests, just to rule out any problems with diabetes or your thyroid, and he might get your heart checked out,' Judith suggested.

'I feel so stupid. It's…' Sylvia sighed. 'My husband left me six months ago. I've been a bit low, and my girls decided to surprise me with a ticket for the Eye, because they knew I wanted to go on it and they thought it might cheer me up. I never dreamed I'd end up…well…' She shook her head. 'Being silly. Ruining your day.'

'You haven't ruined anything,' Kieran said. 'And panic attacks aren't ''being silly''—they're real.'

'Thank you. For rescuing me.'

'Not at all.' Kieran squeezed her hand. 'But Jude's right. When we get off, sit down and have a drink—little sips of cold water, but don't gulp it—then make an appointment at your GP's surgery and have a chat to him.'

'I will. Thank you.'

A few minutes later, they disembarked and walked along the river, arms around each other.

'I'd planned a quietish day,' Kieran said ruefully.

'We had to help her,' Jude pointed out.

'I know. But I meant the Eye to be a kind of appetiser for Paris. I was going to kiss you when we got to the top.'

He held her closer. 'I could try to get tickets for later in the day.'

'It's OK.' She paused. 'You could always kiss me now.'

'Is that an offer?'

'Is that an acceptance?' she fenced.

In answer, Kieran spun her to face him, cupped her face in his hands and brought his lips slowly down to hers. He brushed his mouth against hers, teasing. When she sighed, closed her eyes and opened her mouth, he deepened the kiss. The centre of London faded out, and all Judith was aware of was Kieran's mouth.

When he broke the kiss, she almost fell over. If he hadn't been holding her, she'd have slid into a quivering heap.

He sighed and rested his forehead against hers. 'I had planned to take you on a boat down to Kew Gardens, then go for a wander among the flowers. Lunch by the river. The problem is...all I can think about is you, the other night. Your sofa. Candlelight.'

'And all I can think about is you as a pirate king.' She let her hands drift to his taut backside. 'Wearing faded denims and a black T-shirt.' Just like the ones he was wearing right then. 'All you need is the earring and the hat. Or a bandanna.'

He groaned. 'What was that you were saying about spontaneous combustion?'

'I think we need a taxi,' Judith said. 'Now.'

CHAPTER EIGHT

NEITHER of them spoke on the way back to Judith's house. Kieran held Judith's hand very tightly, as if she were a mirage and he was afraid she'd vanish. Judith returned the pressure of his hand. The journey seemed to take for ever— but then the taxi stopped, Kieran handed the cabbie a note and told him to keep the change, and Judith closed the front door behind them.

At once Kieran pulled her into his arms and kissed her. This time, Judith vowed silently, there would be no inter- ruptions. Nothing and nobody would stop them doing what they'd both wanted to do for days.

She tugged the hem of his T-shirt from the waistband of his jeans and slid her palms against his back, loving the firm muscular feel of his body. In return, Kieran unbuttoned her shirt, caressing her skin as he uncovered it.

And then he stopped.

'What?' Jude mumbled, in a voice she barely recognised as her own, it was so thick with desire.

He rubbed his cheek against hers. 'I'm rushing you.'

'No. I want this, too.'

'We're barely inside your house,' he pointed out.

She shrugged. 'OK, we'll be civilised. My bed's up- stairs.'

He sounded embarrassed. 'There's one other thing. I wasn't actually planning to drag you here and seduce you today.'

He was having second thoughts? Shame flooded through her. They were barely inside her house and she was standing there with her shirt open to the waist. He must think she was a tart.

As if he'd guessed her thoughts, he kissed the corner of her mouth. 'What I mean is I wasn't taking it for granted that we'd make love today. I'm not prepared. I don't have anything with me.'

She relaxed again. 'No need. I'm on the Pill.' She swallowed hard. 'Not that I sleep around. My GP prescribed it because my periods used to be horrendous.'

He pulled back to look into her eyes. 'You didn't need to explain that. I know you're not the type to sleep around. Neither am I.' His eyes were very dark, very intense. 'So it's your call. Would you rather I beat the world land speed record to your local chemist?'

And wait while he bought condoms? 'I can think of better ways to spontaneously combust,' she said huskily.

He smiled. 'Together.'

She nodded, and held out her hand. He took it, and let her lead him upstairs. Judith closed her curtains, and Kieran switched on the bedside light.

'I want to see you,' he said softly.

Her mouth went dry.

Slowly, very slowly, he finished unbuttoning her shirt and slid the soft cotton from her shoulders, pushing her bra straps down at the same time. 'You're so beautiful, Jude,' he told her, his voice husky. 'I want to touch you, taste you.' His mouth traced the line of her clavicle from her right shoulder. He pushed his tongue into the tiny dip at the centre, then kissed all the way along to her left shoulder. He breathed in her scent. 'Mmm. Vanilla. I love your perfume. And your skin's the colour of pure vanilla ice cream.' His head dipped a little further, and then he'd pushed the cup of her bra down until he'd bared her left breast. He traced the edge of her areola with his tongue and she shivered, arching against him.

'I want to touch you, too. Taste you,' she murmured.

He straightened up. 'Pirate wenches aren't supposed to make demands,' he informed her, his eyes glinting.

'Maybe I'm not a pirate's wench. Maybe I'm a pirate myself.'

'Prove it,' he challenged.

'Hands up,' she ordered, lifting her chin.

He shrugged, and did as she'd demanded. She pulled his T-shirt over his head, then undid the top button of his jeans and took a step backwards. 'Mind-blowing,' she breathed.

'You're very, very good for my ego, Jude,' he told her with a grin. And then his smile faded, replaced by pure yearning. 'Come here,' he said softly.

She went into his arms. Matched him kiss for kiss. And when they landed on her bed, skin to skin, she had no idea who'd taken off which piece of clothing or even when. All she was aware of was Kieran. His clean, lemony scent, the softness of his skin against hers, the roughness of the hair on his chest, the feel of his muscular thighs between hers.

'I want you,' she breathed, tilting her pelvis against him. 'Now.'

'Patience,' he said.

'Kieran, don't tease,' she begged.

He kissed her. 'I'm not. I just wanted to see your hair spread over my pillow. Well, *your* pillow,' he amended, playing with her hair. 'Like this.'

'Tease,' she grumbled.

He grinned. 'That's what pirates do.'

'What?'

'Whatever they please.'

'And would it please you to please me?'

'Jude, you talk too much,' he informed her. She was about to protest, but then he entered her—and she couldn't even think any more, let alone talk.

*   *   *

Some time later, she lay on her side, curled into Kieran. Her legs were tangled with his, her cheek rested on his shoulder, and her arm curved across his waist. He held her close, with his cheek resting against her hair.

'I could stay like this for ever,' she whispered.

'Me, too.'

And then her stomach rumbled loudly. Kieran chuckled and dropped a kiss on her hair. 'I know you normally live on take-aways, Jude, but can I assume that you do actually have some food in the house?'

'Yes. Why?'

'Stay here. I'll make us some lunch.' He kissed the tip of her nose and climbed out of bed. 'I had planned to take you to a romantic riverside restaurant. But no way are you leaving that bed for the rest of the afternoon.'

'Back in pirate king mode?' she teased.

He winked as he pulled his jockey shorts on. 'Something like that.'

Judith stared at him in shock. He was actually proposing to go downstairs dressed in only a pair of grey marl jockey shorts? OK, so he was wearing more than you'd see men wearing on a beach or at the swimming pool, but even so…

Her doubts must have been written all over his face, because he chuckled. 'I'll try not to shock your neighbours. But I'm not intending to spend very long in your kitchen.'

And he didn't. It seemed only seconds before he returned carrying a glass, a bottle of sparkling mineral water and a platter of fruit.

'The eggs in your fridge are past sell-by date, or I would have made you an omelette,' he said. 'So your choice is this or this.'

He'd cored and sliced most of the contents of her fruit bowl and her fridge, by the look of it. Peaches, apples, bananas and fresh strawberries.

'This is lovely.'

'Next time,' he said, 'I'll go shopping first and cook you something properly.'

'So there is going to be a next time?'

He frowned. 'Why? Didn't you think there would be?'

Oh, no. She'd spoken aloud. 'Me and my big mouth,' she muttered.

He brushed a kiss across it. 'Perfect mouth, actually.' He held the fruit platter just out of her reach. 'And I'll eat all this by myself unless you explain that remark.'

'The thrill of the chase,' she said.

He frowned. 'I'm still not with you.'

She sighed. 'OK. I told you I've got lousy judgement. And as you know, when I was at med school, I got this reputation for being an ice maiden. Unobtainable. Add to that the fact that I'm Professor Powell's daughter…and there you have a challenge. A target. A scalp ripe for collecting.'

He fed her a slice of peach. 'Has it ever occurred to you that you're so beautiful most men wouldn't think they have a snowflake in hell's chance with you?'

She swallowed the fruit. 'No.'

'Well. Think about it. I nearly didn't ask because of that reason. I thought you just had to be spoken for. And then I discovered that you weren't.' He fed her another piece of fruit. 'So I asked you out. And you turned me down.'

'You know why. Because I got my wires well and truly crossed.'

'Yes.'

'And I've already apologised for that.' She slid a piece of banana into his mouth. 'I told you, I have lousy judgement. I get the good guys wrong as well as the bad.' She sighed. 'So I've always dated the wrong kind of man. The ones who wanted the thrill of the chase, who loved proving to themselves that they could conquer any woman. And as soon as they hooked me, they dumped me.'

He selected a strawberry and brushed it against her lips until she took a bite. 'That doesn't work for me. It wasn't the thrill of the chase that drew me to you. It was just you. And it doesn't matter whose daughter you are either. I want you for yourself.' He ate the other half of the strawberry. 'Just so we're clear on that.'

She picked up a slice of apple. 'It's not surprising I thought you were spoken for. Just look at yourself. You're a consultant, with a degree from Cambridge, nice manners and a sense of humour—and you look like a pirate king, all dark and dangerous and sexy. Everything a woman could wish for. So how come you weren't snapped up years ago?'

'Major personality flaw,' he said lightly, filching a slice of peach.

Judith scoffed. 'I don't buy that for a second. The mums adore you, the dads all want to *be* you, you've got the midwives eating out of your hand and the maternity department's getting rather more visits than usual from the female staff on other wards. Don't you think one of them would have spotted this supposed huge flaw by now?'

He didn't answer.

'Kieran? I'm serious. I told you why I'm single.'

'*Was*,' he corrected.

'Whatever.' She brushed that aside for now. 'So what's your excuse?'

'Maybe I spent too much time on my studies.'

She shook her head. 'That's my line. Anyway, you read medicine at Cambridge. And you're almost too young to be a consultant. QED, you're bright.'

'I still had to study, put my career first.'

'I still don't buy it.'

He was silent for a long, long time. Judith felt a flicker of panic low in her abdomen when she saw his face. It was as if he was struggling with himself, trying to decide if he could tell her something or not. Had she pushed him too far? Was he going to walk away from her right now?

Then he sighed. 'All right. I'll tell you something now that I've never told anyone else—even Tess.'

'And I promise I'll respect your confidence,' she said solemnly.

'Thank you.' Again, he paused for a long time, as if he wasn't sure where to start, or how to get the words out. 'My dad wasn't a very nice man. I adored him when I was little—he always used to play football with me and wrestle with me and taught me to ride a bike, all the things that small boys love. Then I started noticing that my mum cried a lot. I'm not entirely sure why and I haven't wanted to hurt her by asking, but I think he hit her. I know he messed about with other women—I heard the rows. I used to put my head under the blankets but I could still hear them arguing at night when they thought I was asleep. I heard her asking him why she wasn't enough for him and why he wanted other women all the time, then begging him not to leave her. But in the end he left us and went off with another woman. Someone who had older children. So he didn't need either of us any more.'

Judith threaded her fingers through his. 'I'm sorry. That's a lot to cope with when you're a child.' Her fingers tightened against his. 'And if I'd had any idea, I would never, ever have accused you of cheating on your wife.'

'No. I don't suppose you would.' He took a deep breath. 'Anyway, Mum eventually met Martyn. He's a good man—he's made her happy and he's been a good stepfather to me. He even gave me his name. But I'm not Martyn's natural son. I know I've got bad blood in my veins. Blood I don't want to pass on. Which is why, in the past, I've always walked away before things got too serious.' He looked away from her. 'I suppose that's what you might call the thrill of the chase.'

She shook her head. 'That's completely different. The thrill of the chase—that's all about bolstering your ego and dropping someone because you've found another challenge. What you're doing is something else. You're running scared.'

'I probably am.' He looked at her without smiling. 'I saw how my father treated my mother. How it ate away at her confidence until she was a wreck. And I never, ever want to do that to anyone.'

'You won't. If you were the sort to hurt people, regardless, you wouldn't worry about hurting them in the first place.'

'You're ignoring the genetics,' he said tightly. 'My mother picked a man who cheated on her and lied. So did my sister.'

'That's just coincidence.'

'You're not listening to me, Jude. What I'm saying is, no matter how I was brought up, I'm still my father's son.'

She frowned. 'I can't imagine you ever hitting anyone.'

'No?' He disentangled his fingers from hers. 'I thought about it. When Tess told me about Aidan and I realised that he was putting her through exactly what our mother went through…' he grimaced '…I wanted to spread him across the whole of London.'

'You were being protective of your baby sister, and that's understandable. The point is, you might have wanted to hit Aidan, but you didn't actually *do* it.'

Kieran toyed with a piece of fruit. 'You teased me about being a pirate king. But supposing that's what I am, Jude? Supposing that deep down inside I'm like my father—I'll just take what I want and not care who I hurt in the process?'

'I don't think you are.'

'But you don't know it for sure, Jude. I don't know it either.' He sighed. 'I never knew my father's parents so I don't know about my grandfather—but I once heard Mum talking to my aunt. She said my dad's younger brother was exactly the same as him. Cheated on his wife and had heavy fists. He hit his kids as well as his wife. So it runs in the family.' A muscle flickered in Kieran's jaw. 'I suppose I should be grateful that my dad spared me.'

'He didn't spare you,' Judith said softly. 'Physically, yes, but mentally he hurt you.' She knew she was on dangerous ground, but she couldn't leave it now. Not when Kieran had just bared his soul to her. 'Forgive me asking, but was it your choice not to see him?'

'Yes.' He shook his head. 'All right. No. It wasn't at first. He just vanished, until after Mum had met Martyn. Then he suddenly wanted to see me. I'd had enough birthdays and Christmases without even a card from him to know that I couldn't rely on him. I didn't even expect him to turn up that first time. But he did and we went to the zoo. Then he started talking about Mum, and I guessed what was going on. He wanted her back. Not because he wanted her, but because he didn't want anyone else to have her either.' Kieran shrugged. 'After the second or third visit—and more and more pressure on me to try and get Mum back for him—I told Mum I didn't want to go out with Dad again.'

'And you've never seen him since?'

'A couple of times. When I graduated. He was waiting for me outside the college. He wanted to go for a drink with me. Proud father wanting to make a fuss of his doctor son. It was a bit awkward but it was bearable. I thought perhaps he'd changed. Maybe we could salvage some of the mess from the past—maybe we could even be friends.'

'And?' she prompted softly.

'I saw him a couple of times more in London when I was doing my year as a house officer. Then he made a pass at my girlfriend.'

Judith winced. 'Oh, Kieran.'

'She turned him down, and it wasn't that serious between us anyway. But he was the same old Dad—wanted to prove he could pull any woman he chose, and he didn't care whether or not she was involved with someone else, let alone care about the woman he was supposed to be with at the time. It wasn't about hurting me, it was about making himself feel good. And I didn't want to face the fact that my father was a pathetic, lecherous old man—I didn't want to see what I could turn into.'

'So you haven't seen him since?'

'No. And I made sure from then on that none of my relationships were serious. Don't get me wrong—I've never been promiscuous. But right from the start I've always made it clear that I'm looking for fun, not for for ever. And I've always walked away before things got too deep. Before anyone got hurt.'

'Is that a warning?'

'I don't know.' He gave her a half-smile. 'Actually, if you want the truth, this whole thing between us scares me stupid. The way I feel about you...I've never felt like this about anyone else before. I admit I thought that maybe after we'd made love it would be better, that once I'd got the physical thing out of the way I'd be able to think straight again.'

The thrill of the chase, in other words? Judith flinched inwardly.

'But it hasn't worked. If anything, it's made things a lot harder. Because now I know what it's like to hold you, to touch you, to kiss you...I want to be with you all the time. So maybe I ought to walk away now. Not because I don't want you—because I do.'

She couldn't follow his logic. 'That doesn't make sense.'

'I don't want to hurt you, Jude.'

'And you think that it won't hurt me if you walk away?'

'Maybe now, but not as much as if I stay. As I said, there's bad blood in me.'

How could he possibly believe that? She frowned. 'There's a lot of good blood in you, Kieran. Look at what you do for a living—you bring new lives into the world, help people. And what about the way you're looking after Tess?'

'I've made a mess of that, haven't I? I failed to notice that she's got postnatal depression. Worse than that, even though I know about it now, I haven't been able to talk her into doing anything about it.' His eyes were bleak. 'What kind of a man does that make me?'

'We've already been through why you didn't pick it up: because you're so close to the situation it's difficult to look at things objectively. And I can tell you what sort of man you are, Kieran Bailey. A good man. A man who cares.'

'You said yourself, you have lousy judgement.'

'And I've already misjudged you once. Therefore, I'm right now.'

He raised an eyebrow. 'So why haven't I sorted Tess's problems for her?'

'Because you're her big brother. You've probably bossed her about since she was a toddler, so she's used to tuning you out and she just isn't hearing what you're saying.'

'Maybe.'

'There's no maybe about it. You're not your father, Kieran.'

'And you're willing to take that risk?'

She cupped his face in her hands. 'I am, if you are. Because you're not going to hurt me, Kieran. You're not going to lie to me, cheat on me, or make me "the other woman".'

'We're lying now—about us. To Tess.'

'With good reason. And when she's had treatment for her depression, her view of the world will be different.

She'll be able to cope with the idea of sharing you—and she'll be on better terms with your mum and Martyn. She won't feel alone.' She stroked his face and dropped her hands again. 'Your call. Am I worth the risk?'

'Of course you are. I'm just not sure that I am.'

'I'm sure,' she said softly. 'I trust you. And maybe I can teach you to trust yourself.'

CHAPTER NINE

SHE looked so beautiful when she was asleep, Kieran thought. Actually, no. Judith Powell was beautiful all the time. But here, asleep in his arms...this was special. Private. Just the two of them.

And scary.

He'd had bared his soul to her. Told her things he'd never told another living soul. Told her how scared he was that deep inside he was bad news, like his father and his uncle. That he didn't do permanent. And instead of asking him to leave, or being nice about it but cooling off rapidly, Jude had simply held him. Loved him. She'd accepted him, complications and all. She understood that Tess had to be his first priority. She'd even been the one to suggest they should keep their relationship secret until Tess was ready to cope again.

But the fear that prickled down his spine wouldn't go away. Because Jude had also admitted that her judgement in men was terrible. That she always fell for the love-'em-and-leave-'em type. That the last man she'd dated had been cheating on his wife, and she'd been the last to know.

So, logically, if she thought he'd be good for her, the reverse was true.

They'd both got carried away with the moment. And he'd got more than carried away with the idea of romancing her. For her sake, he should walk away. Now. Before he hurt her.

The problem was, he loved her. Loved everything about her. Her sense of the ridiculous, the teasing smile that was never far from her lips, the passion in her eyes when they made love. He loved her hair, the softness of her skin, her voice.

Heart and body and soul, Kieran loved her. He stroked her hair and she nestled closer, murmuring in her sleep. 'I love you, Jude,' he whispered. 'But I'm not good for you.' He'd wanted her so much that he'd ignored the warnings of his conscience. And now he had to face up to what he'd done. Had to do the right thing.

Somehow, he had to find a way to end it without hurting her too much.

Even though it would be like ripping his soul away.

An hour later, he kissed her awake. 'I have to go now,' he said softly.

'Hmm?' She pulled him closer. 'Five more minutes,' she mumbled.

He nuzzled her cheek. 'Jude. I really do have to go.'

Her eyes opened then. They looked almost navy with sleep, like a newborn baby's. And she was as trusting as a baby. How easily he could hurt her.

For her own good, he had to stop this.

Maybe tomorrow. Just let them have one more day together.

'Is it really that late?' she whispered.

He nodded.

She kissed him lightly. 'Thank you for today.'

'It wasn't quite what I'd planned.' A romantic date. Kissing her at the top of the London Eye. Holding her hand on the boat down the river. Walking in a scented garden. Things that could make him forget who he really was.

Instead, he'd dragged her back to her own house. Spent the day in bed with her. Taking his pleasure instead of cherishing her as she deserved.

'I dunno. I thought it worked out rather nicely.' She rubbed the tip of her nose against his. 'My pirate king.'

The king of selfishness. He had nothing to offer her. So he shouldn't have even started this. 'Hey.' He forced a smile to his face. 'If I don't get out of this bed now, I never will.'

'Now, that's a tempting offer.' She smiled back, and stroked his face. 'But we can't snatch any more time today. I know that. So I'm not going to make demands.'

He should feel relieved. He knew that. So why did he feel like such a louse as he climbed out of her bed? Why did he feel as if he was letting Jude down?

She lay back against the pillows and watched him dress. 'Call me tonight?'

'Sure.' He couldn't resist stealing another kiss. Even though he knew he was going to pay dearly for it later. Later, when he'd found the words to explain.

Except he couldn't. When he called her, later that evening, she sang to him. 'Rainy Days and Mondays'. 'Except they don't make me miserable. After today, Monday's my favourite day of the week,' she said.

'Mine, too.' The words were out before he could stop them and he cursed silently. He was supposed to be finding a way of cooling things down, not making them worse by virtually telling her he was head over heels in love with her! He had to start being logical and stop romancing her. Starting now. 'Um, Jude, I've been thinking. I probably can't get away with another late evening this week.'

'Maybe not for just the two of us, but there's Lulu's birthday—we're all going to the Kashmir for a curry after work.' She paused. 'Ask Tess to come along with us. If she doesn't want to leave Charlie, I'm sure he'll have a fine time being cuddled by everyone. You know what maternity staff are like where babies are concerned.'

And although he and Jude wouldn't be alone—wouldn't even be able to acknowledge each other as more than friends—they would at least be together. He could engineer sitting next to her. 'I'll ask her.'

'Just in case she's worried she won't fit in with a bunch of medics, you can tell her we need her help. We have to smuggle the Clooney cut-out from Lulu's office to the Kashmir.'

'Don't tell me you made it this evening?'

'No. But Tess was at art college, right?'

'Ye-es.'

'So she'll know where to get the card from. And how to get the photograph in the right proportions. And it might...' Judith's voice faded, as if she wasn't sure how to say the next bit tactfully.

But Kieran had already followed her line of thought. 'It might give her a purpose, something else to think about, which would help with the depression, if we ask for her help.' Trust Jude to think of that.

'Yes. Um, look, I'm not trying to interfere.'

'I know—and I appreciate it. You're just better than I am at seeing things where my baby sister is concerned. I'll ask her.'

'I'll see you tomorrow, then.'

'Yes.'

'I wish I could kiss you goodnight,' she said. 'Properly. Like this afternoon.'

Tell her. Tell her now. Tell her it has to stop. But his heart wasn't listening to his head. 'Me, too.'

'Kieran?'

'Yes?'

'I know it's too soon. That you're not ready to take a risk. But I—' She paused. 'I like you. I like you a lot.'

His heart contracted when he realised she'd changed her original L-word— to one she thought he might be able to accept. 'Me, too.' More than like. He loved her. Which was why he ought to end it.

But, God help him, he couldn't. He couldn't go back to being detached and lonely and everybody's friend but not having someone who really loved him. Someone he could love back.

And Judith was everything he'd ever wanted.

'I love you,' he whispered, when she'd cut the connection and there was a safe buzz in his ear.

The next day, they were back to being cool, calm, professional colleagues. Nobody in the maternity department would ever have guessed that the previous day their consultant had kissed Judith until she'd been dizzy, made love with her and had told her his deepest, darkest secrets. Kieran treated her just the same as he did everyone else in the team—until she was due for her lunch-break.

'Quick confab in my office first, Jude?' he asked.

'Sure. Do I need any notes?'

Kieran glanced at Louise, then nodded at the pile on the desk. 'Yes. Third one down.'

'Right.'

The moment they were in his office, he drew the blinds and locked the door, then put his finger to his lips. 'I don't need the notes,' he whispered.

'So what did you want to see me about?' she whispered back. Her heart had speeded up a notch. Was he planning to kiss her?

'Lulu's birthday.'

No. Of course he wasn't going to kiss her. Inside the hospital, it was work only. They'd already agreed that. Judith tried to smother her disappointment and hoped it didn't show on her face.

'Tess says we need featherboard—it's like two bits of cardboard sandwiching some foam stuff in the middle. She also says that blowing up a photograph could contravene copyright.'

'But it's only for a bit of fun.' Judith sighed. 'OK, so maybe it isn't going to work.'

'She says she can fix it. And that if it's raining on Thursday night, it'll get soggy, so she's doing something different for the Kashmir.'

'She's coming with us?'

'I think so.'

Judith smiled. 'Brilliant.'

'All credit where it's due. To you.' Kieran took the notes from her hands and placed them on his desk. 'So I owe you something on account.' He took her hands and walked her backwards to his chair. Then he sat down and pulled her onto his lap.

'Kieran, we agreed...'

'I know. But it's driving me crazy, being close to you all day and not being able to touch you. So...' He tipped his head back, offering her his mouth.

She couldn't resist the plea in those dark, dark eyes. She leaned forward and kissed him.

Was this his way of telling her that he was learning to trust? She hoped so. And she hoped that her kiss told him everything she was holding back from saying.

He broke the kiss and traced the outline of her face with his forefinger. 'I'd better let you go before people start to talk. If anyone asks, tell them what Tess is doing.'

'Except Lulu, of course.'

'Except Lulu.' He kissed the tip of her nose. 'Now go. While I can still let you leave.'

To Judith's relief, nobody commented that her eyes were sparkling just that little bit more brightly than normal. And when she told Margot and Daisy about their cardboard cut-out plan—and that Kieran was organising it—they accepted her excuse for being in his office with the blinds drawn and the door shut.

It was shaping up to be their quietest day in months when Judith took the call from Holly. 'I'll be right down,' she said.

Kieran was doing an antenatal clinic so she knew she couldn't ask his advice. She was going to have to stand on her own two feet for once. She patted her pocket to check that her obstetric handbook was to hand, then headed for the emergency department.

'Petunia Barnes, aged thirty-seven, first baby, twenty weeks. Severe abdominal pain, though it doesn't fit the pattern of appendicitis. The portable ultrasound's on the way,' Holly said. 'It's bedlam in here today—we've got three off with a bug—so can I leave you to it?'

'Sure.' Judith took a deep breath and hoped she looked more confident than she felt, then introduced herself to her patient.

'Can you tell me where it hurts?' she asked.

Petunia nodded. 'My tummy.' Her eyes were wide with fear. 'Is my baby going to be all right?'

'Try to relax,' Judith said, holding Petunia's hand. 'As soon as I know what's causing the pain, I'll be able to tell you a lot more. Is there anyone we can call for you?'

Petunia shook her head. 'My husband's at work and they're funny about people taking time off. I just need to know if my baby's all right.'

'The scanner's on its way,' Judith told her. 'Have you noticed any blood at all?'

'No.'

That didn't completely rule out a placental abruption. Sometimes there was a delay before any bleeding appeared.

'Any pain apart from your tummy?'

'No, but I've been feeling a bit funny. I was sick this morning. I thought it was a bug until my stomach started hurting.'

Judith checked Petunia's notes. She had a slight temperature. Petunia also looked more than twenty weeks pregnant. Twins? Or something else?

'Would you mind if I examined you?' Judith asked.

Petunia shook her head. 'Just make the pain stop. Make it be all right.' She winced as Judith palpated her stomach. 'That hurts.'

'I'm sorry. Have you had any knocks to the stomach lately?'

'Nothing. My husband fusses about everything—he'd wrap me in cotton wool if he could. But this *hurts.*'

'OK. I'll go and chase up that scanner, and we'll see what's going on.'

To Judith's relief, the scanner had arrived.

'Have you had an ultrasound before?' she asked.

Petunia shook her head. 'I missed the first one. I'm booked in for Friday.'

'All right. What I'm going to do is put some jelly on your stomach, then put the scanning head across your tummy. It's not going to hurt the baby at all—it'll just bounce back sound waves, and the jelly helps to amplify the waves so we get a better picture. Here we go.' She turned the screen so Petunia could see it. 'Say hello to your baby.'

'It's all right?'

'The heart's beating normally—that's the dark area here—and here's the bladder. This dark area here's your placenta.' It looked fine—no sign of an abruption or any hidden bleeding. And then Judith saw a mass in the body of the uterus.

'Does it hurt here?' she asked, gently palpating Petunia's abdomen around the area of the mass.

'Yes.'

'Has anyone in your family ever had fibroids?'

Petunia nodded. 'My sister.'

'That's what's causing your pain,' Judith said.

'I thought they didn't hurt?'

'Often they don't—but they can cause backache, heavy or painful periods, and painful sex. I take it, as your sister has them, you know a fibroid is a benign tumour of muscular and fibrous tissue?'

Petunia nodded.

'They tend to grow bigger during pregnancy.' Fibroids were also more common in women of Afro-Caribbean descent, like Petunia, and in women aged over thirty-five. 'What's happened here is that the fibroid grew so quickly that it needed more blood supply than it could get. So the tissue in the centre of the fibroid died, and it's started bleeding in the middle. It's what we call ''red degeneration'' because the fibroid will look red.'

'Is it going to hurt my baby?'

'Fibroids can cause miscarriage, yes,' Judith said, 'but generally they tend to rise away from the pelvis, so it shouldn't cause you a problem in labour.'

'Will you have to take it out?'

'We'll need to do something about it after you've had the baby, but it doesn't necessarily mean an operation. We can do keyhole surgery on fibroids nowadays—we simply cut off its blood supply and it shrinks.' Judith smiled at her. 'But for now, we need to stop the pain. The good news is, it generally clears up in less than a week, with painkillers and bed-rest.'

'So I'm not going to lose the baby?'

'I don't think so. But if you're worried at any time, call your midwife or the maternity unit. I'll write you up for some painkillers.'

Petunia wiped away a tear. 'I was so scared I was going to lose the baby. The pain's so bad.'

'I know. But we can stop that.' Judith smiled at her. 'And you've seen the baby now. The heartbeat's fine. Have you felt any movements yet?'

'Should I have done?'

'It's your first baby, so you might not have noticed anything yet. At first, it's like someone's blowing bubbles into a glass.' Judith winked. 'Give it another ten weeks, and you'll be awake at three in the morning while the baby's practising gymnastics.'

Petunia smiled back. 'Thank you. For…well, stopping me worrying.'

'That's what I'm here for. Any time.'

Funny, Judith thought after her antenatal clinic had finished. This was the first time she hadn't double-checked things in her obstetric handbook. Maybe she was starting to trust her instincts.

Because of Kieran.

Because he believed in her.

And maybe, just maybe, he'd come to realise that she believed in him, too.

The following day, Jude was delighted to sign the discharge form for Sara Cox. 'The baby's going to be in Special Care for another three or four days,' Sara said, 'but he's going to be all right. Thank you for all you did, Jude.'

Judith smith and shook her head. 'It's not me you need to thank. Kieran was the one who did the section.'

'And you were the one who spotted vasa praevia before it was too late,' a voice murmured in her ear. 'So take the credit where it's due.'

The touch of Kieran's breath against her skin made her shiver. 'Ha. Normally listeners never hear any good of themselves,' she told him.

'Don't make me pull rank,' he retorted with a grin. 'I just wanted to call in and wish you all the best, Sara. And to ask you to bring little Micky down to see us before you go.'

'I will,' she promised.

*   *   *

On Thursday, Jude came in an hour before the start of her shift to help decorate Louise's office. She kept half an eye on the clock as she blew up balloons and draped streamers everywhere. If Kieran didn't turn up before Louise got there, she'd have to find a string of excuses to keep the senior midwife well away from her office.

He made it with about three minutes to spare. 'Where's the cut-out?' she asked.

'Here. I need a hand with the wrapping.'

They stripped the bubble-wrap and brown paper from the six-foot-high cut-out, and Judith's jaw dropped. 'I know you said Tess went to art college, but I had no idea she was this good.' Kieran's sister hadn't used a photograph at all. She'd drawn the face onto the featherboard. And it was a perfect likeness of the actor Louise adored. 'I'll tell her so tonight.'

Kieran grinned. 'Good. She says we need to put scrubs on him.'

'Lulu's going to be here any moment. Go and distract her.'

'How?'

'Use your imagination!' she said, glowering at him.

'That particular form of distraction,' he said softly, 'is reserved. I'll go and get the others to sing ''Happy Birthday'' or something.'

Five minutes later, the cut-out was adorned in green scrubs. Judith moved the flap at the back to keep it standing upright, then sidled out of the senior midwife's office.

'What are you up to, Dr Powell?' Louise asked suspiciously.

'Just leaving you a little present. Happy birthday, Lulu.' Judith hugged her friend.

'I take it you were responsible for those balloons?' Louise asked, nodding at the string down the corridor which spelt out HAPPY 40TH, LULU.

'Well, you didn't think we'd let it pass quietly, did you?'

Louise grinned. 'Just remember that you've got a big birthday coming up later this year, too.'

The whole team gathered outside Louise's office.

'I've got a nasty feeling about this,' Louise said. 'What have you lot been up to?'

Judith opened the door and ushered her friend inside. 'Just this.'

Louise stared at the cut-out.

'That's a first. Our Lulu, silent,' Judith teased.

'I'm just...overwhelmed. That's...mine?'

'You wanted him with a ribbon round his neck,' Daisy reminded her.

Louise read out the label. '"Happy Fortieth, with love from all on Maternity." Wow, Jude—I didn't know you could draw.'

'Not me,' Judith explained. 'Kieran's sister.'

'So you brought this in—hang on, aren't you supposed to be on a day off?' Louise asked, looking at Kieran.

'Well. It's not every day your favourite midwife turns forty,' he said with a grin.

'I think I'm going to cry,' Louise said.

'Not until you've shared your chocolates,' Daisy said.

'And opened your presents,' Margot added.

'And these were delivered about thirty seconds ago,' Kieran said, handing Louise an enormous bouquet.

'I'm—I'm overwhelmed,' Louise said, smiling through her tears. 'Thank you. All of you.'

'We haven't finished yet,' Judith warned with a grin. 'There's still tonight...'

Kieran was waiting at the Kashmir when Judith, Louise and the others finished their shift.

'Where's Tess?' Judith mouthed.

'Changed her mind,' he mouthed back.

They didn't get the chance to discuss it in the Indian restaurant, even though Kieran managed to get a seat right next to Judith's, because everyone was talking and laughing so loudly. Particularly when Louise discovered Tess's final surprise: she'd photocopied the face from the cut-out onto thin card and had made a mask for everyone except Louise.

'It's got to be every woman's dream date. You and ten George Clooneys,' Margot said, laughing.

Just me and Kieran would do, Jude thought.

He was very quiet that evening. Clearly, he was worried about Tess.

'Why don't you go early?' Jude asked him softly.

'I don't want to spoil Lulu's birthday.'

'You won't be. Look, I'll ring your mobile from the loos. Tell everyone Charlie's not well, and they'll all understand.'

'More lies.'

'White ones. With the best intentions,' she reminded him.

'I was going to walk you home.'

'There'll be other nights,' she promised. She slipped out to the toilets, and thirty seconds later Kieran's mobile phone shrilled.

'Sorry—I'm going to have to be a party-pooper. Charlie's not well,' Kieran said. He gave Margot some notes from his wallet. 'That should cover my share of the meal—and buy everyone a drink for me, will you?'

'Of course I will,' the midwife promised.

Kieran kissed Louise's cheek. 'Happy birthday, old girl,' he said with a grin.

'You cheeky young whipper-snapper,' she retorted, laughing. 'And, please, thank your sister for everything. I'm thrilled to bits with all my gorgeous Georges.'

The corridor to the toilets was next to the exit, and before Judith had a chance to return to the table, he swept her back into the corridor. 'Thank you,' he said.

'I'll call you later,' she promised.

'What I would give for just ten minutes in your arms,' Kieran said, his voice tortured.

'I know. But we can't right now.' She kissed him lightly. 'Now, go.'

When Kieran arrived home, Tess was slumped listlessly on the sofa in front of the television. She wasn't even watching it, he realised.

'OK?' he asked, knowing that she wasn't.

'Yeah.'

So she hadn't noticed that he was home early. And she didn't ask if he'd had a good time. Or what anyone thought of her artwork. The spark he'd seen the day before, when she'd been drawing, was well and truly extinguished. 'Lulu loved your cut-out. And I think half the nurses in the hospital are sick with jealousy because they want one, too,' Kieran said.

'Oh.'

'Everyone sends their love. They missed you tonight. Lulu wanted to thank you herself.'

She shrugged. 'I didn't feel up to it.'

Kieran sat next to her and took her hand. 'Tess, I'm worried about you. I know you've been feeling low lately.'

'I'm all right.'

'You're not, sweetheart. And that's not a criticism of you—you've had a hell of a lot to cope with lately. I just think you need some help. Go and see your GP. Tell him how you've been feeling. He'll be able to give you something.'

Tess shook his hand away. 'I never thought you'd be the sort who'd say a little pill will cure everything.'

'It won't. But you're clinically depressed, Tess. A short course of antidepressants won't make you addicted. They won't solve all your problems, but they'll help you get back on an even keel and make you feel as if you can cope again.'

'Right. And Charlie will go on an at-risk register.'

'He's more likely to do that if you *don't* get help,' Kieran said bluntly.

She glared at him. 'Is all this because I didn't come with you tonight?'

'Partly. Look, you know I love you. You're my baby sister and I've adored you since I first met you when you were thirty minutes old with a squidgy red face. I just want to help you.'

'And make me take drugs? No, thanks. I'm not like Aidan.'

Kieran frowned. 'What's he got to do with it?'

'Nothing.'

'Was he an addict? Is that it?'

Tess folded her arms and refused to answer.

'Tess, if you don't want to talk to me, I understand. But you need to talk to someone.'

'I'm all right.'

He put his arms round her. 'Just some days you're more all right than others.'

'You're nagging me.'

'Because I care. Trust me. I've been around enough new mums to know the signs.'

'You never said anything before.'

'I was in denial. I'm not now.'

She shrugged him off. 'All right. If you must know, Aidan used to take Ecstasy. Before you ask, no, I never did. But I don't want to spend my life on pills.'

'You won't. It's just a short course. Just enough to make you feel a bit less overwhelmed.'

'Enough to stop my big brother nagging me?'

He hugged her. 'No chance. That's what big brothers are for. But, please, Tess, just talk to someone. Promise me?'

She sighed. 'All right. I'll go and see the doctor.'

'And I'll try not to nag. Well, not as much,' he amended.

And once Tess was on an even keel again…maybe then he'd be able to get things straight in his head about Judith. Work out if they really had a future. And if he dared to open his heart to her.

CHAPTER TEN

'I CAN'T stand this itching,' Letitia said, rubbing at her hands. 'It's driving me bananas. My midwife said pregnant women get a bit itchy, especially in hot weather, but this is keeping me awake all night. So she sent me here.'

'How long has the itching been going on?' Judith asked.

'About a week. I can't take much more of it. My husband gets eczema and he said I ought to use his cream, but I didn't want to risk it in case it hurt the baby.'

'Emollients are fine—you might find that aqueous cream helps. Have lots of tepid baths, try to keep as cool as you can, wear cotton and avoid wool, try calamine lotion or rub your skin very gently with a baby's hairbrush. But I expect you already know all that,' Judith said wryly. 'Is the itching anywhere in particular?'

'My hands.'

Warning bells started to ring in Judith's head. 'Have you got a rash anywhere?'

Letitia shook her head. 'So what's causing it?'

'I'll need to do a couple of blood tests to find out,' Judith said, 'but it could well be something called obstetric cholestasis.'

'And in English, that means?'

'A liver problem. We don't actually know what causes it, but it's possible that your liver isn't coping with the high levels of pregnancy hormones, so it's not doing its normal job. Your liver makes bile, to help your intestine digest your food—but with obstetric cholestasis the bile flows too slowly, so it builds up in your bloodstream and causes the itching. Is it worse at night?'

'Is it ever!' Letitia pulled a face.

'Did you bring me a urine sample?'

'Yes. At twenty-eight weeks, I've got it down to a fine art,' Letitia said. She fished in her handbag for the little sample tube. 'Here.'

The urine was dark, Judith noted as she tested it for sugar and protein. 'OK, Letitia. How are you with needles?'

'If you can stop the itch, you can stick a hundred needles in me,' Letitia said feelingly.

Judith chuckled. 'It's not going to be that bad. I'm going to take a blood sample and send it for liver function tests and serum bile tests. I'm also going to do a test for viral hepatitis and send you for a scan, just in case it's gallstones.'

'What happens then?'

'If it's obstetric cholestasis, certain chemicals will be raised.' Namely bile acids, bilirubin, serum alkaline phosphatase and enzymes known as transaminases.

'And you can give me something for it?'

Judith nodded. 'We can give you something called ursodeoxycholic acid. It hasn't been licensed for use in pregnancy, simply because it hasn't undergone the usual rigorous testing, but studies show that it helps stop the itch and brings the liver function back to near normal.'

'And it won't hurt the baby?'

'All the studies so far say it won't. But, as I said, ursodeoxycholic acid isn't licensed for use in pregnancy, so if you want to try it you'll need to sign a consent form.'

'I'll go mad if I keep itching like this,' Letitia groaned.

'If you want to see the consultant and talk it through with him, I can arrange it,' Judith said.

'No. You sound as if you know your stuff. I'll sign the form.'

'OK. Though obviously I can't give it to you until we've got the results of the liver tests back. We'll also need to give you a tablet of vitamin K, to make sure that your blood's clotting properly before you give birth.'

'What about the baby? Is it going to affect him?'

'If we don't treat the obstetric cholestasis, there's a risk you'll go into labour early, that the baby might be in distress, or even that you might have a stillbirth. But if we know about the problem, we can keep a close eye on you— we might suggest giving you steroids to help mature the baby's lungs, then induce you at around thirty-seven weeks.'

Letitia looked thoughtful. 'Is it very common?'

'No. It affects one or two in a thousand. And it's nothing you did, though there's a chance your mum or your sister or your grandmother might have had it.'

'If I have another baby, will I get this again?'

'It's fairly likely,' Judith told her. 'But at least we know about it and can keep a check on you. It doesn't usually leave any lasting damage, though you may find that you start itching when you ovulate or just before your period starts. '

'What about if the tests come back clear?'

'Sometimes you start itching before it shows in the liver tests. If they're clear but you're still itching, we'll test you again,' Judith reassured her. 'The itching should stop within a couple of weeks after the birth, but you'll need to look at the sort of birth control you want to use—oestrogen-based oral contraceptives can cause a bit of a problem.' She took the blood samples and labelled them. 'I'll just check your blood pressure and the baby's heartbeat.' She quickly put the cuff of the sphygmomanometer on Letitia's arm and began to pump it up. 'Yep, that's pretty good.'

'And itchy,' Letitia grumbled.

Judith soaked a paper towel in water, squeezed the excess water off and handed it to Letitia. 'For the time being,' she said with a smile.

'Just knowing I don't have to put up with this for much longer makes it better.'

'Of course it does. I'll ring you as soon as the results are through. Are your contact numbers still the same?'

'Yes.'

'Good.' She bared Letitia's abdomen. 'I take it you'd like to hear the heartbeat as well?'

Letitia nodded.

'Good. Because I really, really hate using the Pinard stethoscope. The Sonicaid's so much clearer.' She put the transponder against Letitia and the quick, steady beat of the baby's heart filled the room. 'Sounds good.' She palpated Letitia's abdomen. 'And it feels as if the baby's progressing nicely for dates.' Judith smiled as Letitia restored order to her clothes. 'I'll ring you when the results are back, but if you're worried about anything in the meantime, ring your midwife or call the ward and ask for me.'

The rest of Judith's antenatal clinic went swiftly. She was on her way back up to the ward when she saw Kieran coming towards her.

'You're due a break, aren't you?'

She nodded.

'Have lunch with me?'

'Sure.'

'If anyone sees me gazing into your eyes, I'll tell them I'm fascinated with one of your case histories,' he said with a grin.

'Actually, I do have one—a possible case of obstetric cholestasis.' She gave him a brief run-through.

'Isn't your dad doing a trial on ursodeoxycholic acid?'

'Yes. I might refer her to him, actually—depending on the test results, and if Bella doesn't mind.'

'I'm sure she won't.'

They bought sandwiches in the café, then found a quiet table in the corner.

'So how's your day been?' she asked.

'OK.'

'But?'

He sighed. 'Tess. I nagged her into seeing her GP. She wasn't very happy about it but she finally agreed to go. Now she won't tell me what he said or show me what he prescribed her. If anything, she's got snappier with me than before she went.'

'Probably because you're fussing too much,' Judith said. 'You're being paranoid. Let her tell you when she's ready—if you put pressure on her, she's less likely to talk to you.'

'How did you get to be so wise?' he asked.

'About siblings, when I'm an only child?' She grinned. 'Because I get to hear all the sob stories from my friends.'

'Right.' He slid one foot between hers. 'Mmm. That's better.'

Actually, it wasn't. Because it wasn't nearly enough. 'When's your next day off?' she asked.

'Friday. Yours?'

'Tomorrow.'

He sighed. 'Somehow we need to co-ordinate our off-duty days. But if we change them, someone's bound to notice that we're off together—and guess that we planned it that way.'

'Patience,' she counselled.

'It's not my strong suit.'

'It's not for long. Just until Tess is coping better and won't feel threatened by me.' She bit her lip. 'I did ask her if she wanted to go for a pizza with me, Zo and Holls—when she came in with Charlie, I mean. Maybe I ought to ring her... But I don't want her thinking that I was just using her to get to you, when we tell her about us.'

'Now who's being paranoid?' he asked wryly.

'I suppose.' She smiled at him. 'Are you coming to the fundraiser next week?'

'If you promise to sing something for me.'

'"Rainy Days and Mondays",' she said with a grin. 'Bring Tess with you.'

'I will.' He paused. 'Are you busy tonight?'

'Why?'

'We're both on an early. I wondered if you fancied trying one of my world-famous omelettes.'

'Small problem. Somebody threw my eggs out last week.'

'Eggs that were past their sell-by date,' he reminded her. 'They'd be suppurating by now.'

'No eggs, no omelette.'

'I suppose you wouldn't have any rocket either. Or vine tomatoes. Or apple balsamic vinegar.'

'You are *such* a food snob,' she said, laughing.

Kieran laughed back. 'Jude, anyone who doesn't live on take-aways is a food snob in your book.'

'What's this about food snobs?' a voice asked beside them, and they both jumped.

'You'll be on my side, Margot. Tell her that her diet's unhealthy. She can't preach to our mums when she lives on junk,' Kieran protested.

'By rights,' Margot said, 'with what she eats, she ought to be the size of six houses. But she's not. So she can get away with it.'

Judith breathed on her nails, polished them on her sleeve and pulled a face at Kieran. 'See?'

'Ha.' He glanced at his watch. 'I'd better get back to the ward. Let me know if you need a second opinion on those liver function tests.'

'Will do. See you later.' Judith sketched a salute to him, then smiled at Margot. 'So was it a boy or girl?'

'Girl. And she was *gorgeous*.'

'Margot, you say that about *all* your babies,' Judith pointed out. 'Even the ones with forceps marks.'

'That's because they're all gorgeous.' The midwife smiled back at her. 'Liver function tests? Sounds like you had a mum in clinic with obstetric cholestasis.'

'Suspected.' Judith nodded. 'But our revered consultant insisted on having lunch before he'd talk about my proposed treatment plan.'

'Fair dues, Jude. He's been on for five hours without a break.'

'And you must have been in the delivery room for six.' Judith grimaced. 'Which means I'm a total slacker, compared to you two, so I'd better get back to the ward.' Right now. Before she said something incriminating about Kieran. She only hoped that Margot hadn't overheard their conversation immediately before Kieran's remark about food snobbery. One word in the wrong place, and the whole thing could explode.

'I've taken up gym membership,' Kieran informed Judith on the phone that evening.

'Since when?'

'Since it buys me time with you. An hour for a workout.'

She collapsed in giggles. 'That's one word for it, I suppose.'

Kieran suddenly realised what he'd said. 'Oh, hell. I didn't mean it like that. I meant an hour I could spend at the gym, plus travelling time, means an hour I can spend with you, plus travelling time. I'll run home from yours, so I can truthfully say I've been pounding the deck.'

'Just not at the gym. Kieran, I hate all these lies.'

'So do I. But what else can we do?'

'I suppose. So when are you training tomorrow?'

'About the same time you get off your shift. Meet you

at your place?' His voice softened. 'And I'll cook you that omelette.'

'The omelette that very nearly got us into trouble today,' she reminded him.

'Did Margot say anything?'

'No. But I don't think we should have lunch together again. Not on our own anyway. It's not safe—we'll start making mistakes.'

He groaned. 'This is driving me crazy.'

'Me, too,' she said softly.

'You're on an early tomorrow, aren't you?'

'Yes.'

'Then I'll see you at six. With my six-pack. Of eggs, that is.'

Judith chuckled. 'So you're not really telling lies. It's just…semantics.'

'Eggs-actly.'

She groaned. 'That's terrible. I'm going.'

'Jude?' He paused. 'I…' *I love you.* He couldn't say it. In case it made everything go wrong. 'I'll see you tomorrow.'

Somehow Judith managed to keep her mind on her job the following day. And then her shift was over. She almost ran home. Showered. Changed. And three minutes later, her doorbell rang.

'Dinner is served. Or it will be in ten minutes,' Kieran promised.

'Make that twelve,' Judith said as she closed the door. 'First…' She kissed him.

Time stopped. Her senses were filled with Kieran, the way he touched her, the way he tasted, his clean male scent, the sound of his heartbeat. And if she opened her eyes, she knew all she'd be able to see was Kieran.

'You drive me crazy, Jude,' he whispered as he broke

the kiss. 'And I haven't got time to make love to you the way you really deserve.'

I'd settle for a quickie.

Then her face burned. She really, really hoped she hadn't said that aloud. It made her sound too needy, too desperate. And, given what he'd already told her about leaving before things got too deep, she had to play this cool. 'You were going to make me an omelette.'

'Not just an omelette.' He slid his arm round her shoulders and shepherded her into her kitchen. 'Are we eating here?'

'Unless you want me to set the table in the dining room?'

'Here's fine.'

She sat on one of the chairs next to the small mosaic-topped table in her kitchen and watched as he started removing things from his gym bag.

'Isn't that meant to be for your gym kit?'

'That's in there, too.' He gave her a little-boy grin that made her glad she was sitting down. Her knees definitely went weak. 'I made our first course at my place.'

'Didn't Tess notice?'

'I made some for her, too.' He opened her freezer and slid a package inside, set out the rest of the things he'd bought from the supermarket, then took out a sealed plastic box. 'Where's your crockery?'

'Top right-hand cupboard,' she directed. 'Are we having white or red wine?'

'White.'

'New Zealand OK?'

'More than OK.'

'There's a bottle chilling in the fridge.' There usually was, on the off chance that Holly or Zoe would pop round. But, please, not tonight. Or at least not until Kieran's left, she begged inwardly. 'I'll open it. How do you want me to set the table?'

'Three courses.'

And this was meant to be a quick meal?

But two minutes later they were sitting down with a glass of wine and a plateful of prawns mixed with mango, on a bed of baby oak-leaf lettuce.

'This smells gorgeous,' Judith said.

'It's marinaded in ginger, garlic, lime and a little *nam pla*. Thai fish sauce,' he added, seeing the puzzlement in her face.

'Mmm. And it tastes as good as it smells,' she said after the first mouthful.

'It gets better. I promise.'

She watched as he whipped up a soufflé omelette filled with mushrooms and blue cheese. While the top of the omelette was setting and the cheese was bubbling under the grill, he sliced some vine tomatoes and spread them over a bed of rocket, added a drizzle of balsamic vinegar and oil, then set some Italian rosemary bread and a small dish of olive oil on the table.

Judith closed her eyes in bliss at the first taste. 'This is wonderful. I could get used to healthy food.' Especially if he was the one to cook it for her.

'It's faster than a take-away, too.'

Which didn't mean she wanted to do it for herself. A sandwich was her limit, and even then she'd rather buy one than fuss around slicing things and spreading things and using time she could spend at the piano. 'I can't believe you brought your own omelette pan with you.'

'Have you got one?' he asked.

She grinned. 'What do you think?'

'Exactly.' He raised an eyebrow. 'Maybe I can teach you to cook. Teach you that it can be fun, not just a chore.'

'Maybe we can teach each other a lot of things,' she said softly.

He reached across the table and took her hand. 'Maybe.'

The omelette was followed by fresh raspberries and best-quality vanilla ice cream.

'Bliss. This is as good as Zoe's home-made ice cream,' Judith pronounced.

'I'm not claiming that. Though I do a mean chocolate mousse.'

Judith beamed at him. 'Next time. That's a definite.'

She made coffee afterwards and rummaged in the fridge. 'Now, *this* is the kind of fast food I really like,' she said, setting the tiny gold-wrapped parcels on a plate. 'I think even you might agree that it's good.'

'What is it?'

'Wait and see. Let's go and sit in the living room.' He carried the tray in while she lit vanilla-scented candles. She sat on one corner of the sofa and patted the seat next to her. 'After cooking me that fabulous meal, I think you deserve a head massage.'

'Sounds good to me.' He lay down with his head in her lap and let her fingertips massage the tension away from his scalp.

'The suspense is killing me. What's in those parcels?' he murmured drowsily.

'Keep your eyes closed,' Judith directed. She leaned forward and unwrapped a piece of gianduja. 'Now open your mouth.' He did, and she popped the gianduja into his mouth.

Kieran's tastebuds were in heaven. In fact, Kieran thought he probably *had* died and gone to heaven. Lying here like this with the woman who occupied rather more of his mind than she ought to do, this was the perfect way to wind down at the end of the week.

The chocolate was good, too.

But he'd settle for just Jude.

'OK, I admit it's fabulous,' he said softly when he'd finished the chocolate. 'What is it?'

'Gianduja. Otherwise known as toasted hazelnuts and cocoa butter.'

He grinned and opened his eyes again. Trust his beautiful junk-food addict to pick something like this. 'I might have guessed you couldn't really class it as healthy. And before you start quoting the health benefits of monounsaturated fat at me, I think the cocoa butter definitely cancels out the hazelnuts. It's not the seventy per cent solids stuff.'

'Spoilsport. I'll have to eat it all myself, then,' she threatened. But her eyes were laughing.

And this, Kieran realised, was what he wanted for the rest of his life. To be with Judith. He wanted to live with her, love her, grow old with her. 'Sing something for me?' he asked.

'Any requests?'

'I don't mind. I just love hearing you sing.'

She stroked his cheek and he captured her hand, pressing a kiss into her palm and folding her fingers over it.

And then at last she began to sing. A slow, haunting, a cappella version of 'The First Time Ever I Saw Your Face'. He'd heard the song before, but this was the first time it had ever meant anything. The first time it had moved him so much that there were tears in his eyes when she finished.

There were tears in her eyes, too. Tears of longing and wistfulness. Of something her face said she really wanted to say, but was holding back for his sake.

He shifted to a sitting position, so he could look into her eyes properly. What she'd just sung was the most beautiful song he'd ever heard. And she'd meant every single word. It was her way of saying the words that were straining at his own heart. The words he needed to say, right here, right now. And to hell with the risks.

'Jude. That was…' His voice cracked and he shook his

head. 'It was incredible. *You're* incredible.' He cupped her face. 'I...I'm not sure how to say this.'

Fear flickered in his eyes and he could tell that her breathing had become shallow. Worried. 'I'm listening,' she said. The words were cool, but her voice had a slight tremor.

She thought he was going to leave her.

For her sake, maybe he *should* leave her.

But, heaven help him, he couldn't. He wanted her too much.

'I...' He was talking through sand. The words wouldn't come out. Why couldn't she just be a mind-reader and know what he wanted to say?

His thumb caressed the corner of her mouth. 'I love you, Jude,' he breathed.

He kissed her, pouring his soul into the kiss, wanting her to know just how deeply he felt it. And when he broke the kiss, he realised his face was wet. 'You're crying,' he whispered. 'Don't cry.'

'I'm not crying because I'm sad,' she told him. 'It's because...'

'I know.' He held her close. 'I've never felt like this. I've never wanted for ever before. But now I do. I want it with you.'

'Me, too. I love you, Kieran.'

'We'll have for ever,' he promised. 'One day. Soon.'

CHAPTER ELEVEN

IN THE meantime, they had to take snatched moments wherever they could get them. An hour here, a phone call there, a note sneaked into Kieran's briefcase or Judith's locker.

On Monday morning, Judith got Letitia's liver function test results. A quick confab with Bella meant that the obstetric director gave her permission to talk to her father about the ursodeoxycholic acid trial, so she rang his office at the Hampstead Free.

'Hello, darling. You don't usually ring me at work. Everything all right?' Ben asked.

'Yes, of course it is. Can't I ring my favourite professor because I feel like it?' she teased.

Ben chuckled. 'I've always got time for my favourite daughter. Business or pleasure?'

'Business, actually. I've got a mum you might like to see for your ursodeoxycholic acid trial.'

'Right. I've got a pen. Fire away.'

Judith gave her father all the details. 'I'll ring her this morning and ask her to call you.'

'Do that, darling. How are you getting on with Kieran?'

Judith froze. Had her father heard any gossip about them? No, of course not. Kieran was a former colleague and her father was just interested in how he'd settled into his new post. 'Fine,' she said. 'Actually, he's really easy to work with.'

'He's a good man.' Ben paused. 'Are you singing again soon?'

'Dad, if you looked at Mum's calendar yourself, instead of relying on her to tell you things,' Judith said, laughing, 'you'd know it's this Wednesday. I've already fleeced her for tickets.'

'Wednesday? Oh, darling. I'm not going to be able to make this Wednesday. I've got a trust meeting. Your mother might still come.'

'Hey, no worries. It's just a fundraiser.'

'Yes, but it's my daughter singing,' Ben pointed out. 'Next time, I promise, I'll be there. I know I haven't made it to any of your fundraisers for a while.'

'You're a busy man, Dad. And you're not missing that much. You heard me sing around the house enough when I was younger.'

'Even so.' He sighed. 'I'd better let you go. Love you, darling.'

'Love you, too, Dad. See you soon.'

Kieran stopped in the corridor as he heard her words. *Love you too, Dad.*

He hadn't said that for well over twenty years.

His father had always fished for the words at the end of his visits. 'Love you, son.' Except Kieran hadn't really believed him and had refused to say it back. If his dad had really loved him, he wouldn't have walked out on his only child without explaining at least enough to make the little boy realise it wasn't his fault. Tom Galloway wouldn't have ignored birthdays and Christmases, not even bothering to send a card. He would have made the effort to ring his son and see how things were going, taken an interest in his schoolwork, listened to his dreams.

But he hadn't.

And Martyn, although he'd tried his best to make Kieran feel like his real son, had always been that little bit apart. 'Martyn', not 'Dad'. Now Kieran thought about it, he couldn't remember the last time he'd told his mother or his stepfather that he loved them. Just Tess. Maybe it was because his little sister was younger than he was. She'd always been vulnerable in his eyes so it was safe to say it to her.

I love you, too.

Jude found it so easy to say. She was comfortable talking about emotions. Whereas he… Since the moment he'd admitted that he loved her, he hadn't been able to say it again. Hadn't been able to tell her the words he knew she wanted to hear.

'You are the most pathetic man in the universe,' he informed himself roughly. Tonight. He'd tell her again tonight. And mean every single word.

On the evening of the fundraiser, Kieran came home expecting to see Tess dressed up ready for a night out, but she was still wearing scruffy leggings and a T-shirt Charlie had dribbled food over. Breakfast *and* lunch, by the look of it. Her hair didn't look as if it had seen a brush since she'd got up either.

'Do you want the shower first?' he asked.

'What do you mean?'

'It's the fundraiser tonight.'

Tess shook her head. 'I'm not going. I need to stay with Charlie.'

'Rosemary said she'd babysit. You know he'll be safe with her. And you haven't been out for ages, Tess.'

She scowled. 'Don't nag.'

He frowned. He knew it took time for antidepressants to kick in, but he'd expected to see some kind of lift in her mood by now. A nasty suspicion flicked at him. 'You *are* taking the antidepressants, aren't you?'

'Oh, will you get off my case? You're worse than Mum!'

'Only because I care.'

'Care?' Tess shook her head. 'You're stifling me, Kieran.'

The weeks of worry and treading carefully suddenly boiled over. 'OK. If that's the way you feel, I'll go on my own. And I don't know what time I'll be back, because I'm going to help Jude, Holly and Zoe clear up.' Thin-lipped, he strode upstairs to have a shower and change, and he didn't bother saying goodbye—simply slammed the door as he left.

But by the time he got to the hospital social club, Kieran was feeling sick with guilt. Tess was ill. He should be treating her with kid gloves, not yelling at her. He pulled his mobile phone out of his pocket and rang home. As he half expected, the answering-machine clicked in. And she didn't pick up the phone. No doubt she was still too angry with him to talk to him. Or maybe she was giving Charlie a bath and hadn't heard the phone ring.

Time for damage limitation. If he apologised now, at least she'd get the message and have time to simmer down again by the end of the evening. 'Tess, it's me,' he said after the long beep. 'I'm sorry. I was mean to you. Let's talk when I get back.' He cut the connection and went into the little room where Judith was running soundchecks.

'Anything I can do to help?' he asked Holly.

She shook her head. 'Just enjoy it, really.'

'I'll help clear up, if you like.' At her surprise glance, he added hastily, 'To support my registrar, seeing as we're getting a third of the proceeds.'

Holly smiled. 'Cheers. I'll hold you to that.'

As usual, Judith was brilliant. But Kieran couldn't relax and enjoy it. Everything was too mixed up inside—how much he wanted to be with Jude, how mean he'd been to Tess. And how, despite what Jude said, his father's genes were coming through loud and clear—because the minute something had stopped him getting what he wanted, he'd been nasty about it.

'Where's Tess?' Judith asked Kieran when her set had finished and she came to help clear up.

'Changed her mind,' he said shortly.

'That's a pity.'

When he didn't respond, she frowned. 'Are you all right?'

'Fine.'

'What's the real story?'

He sighed. He should have guessed that she'd know something was wrong. 'We had a fight. I did try ringing her earlier, to apologise, but she wouldn't answer the phone.'

'Hey. Why don't you go home and make it up with her?'

'I said I'd help here. And I wanted to walk you home.'

'No need. Remember, Holls lives next door to me. I can go home with her.' Judith put some brownies into a bag. 'Take these as a peace offering and go and sort it out.' She lifted one hand to silence his protest. 'There's plenty of people here to help, so don't feel guilty.'

'I'll call you later,' he promised.

'If you can. Otherwise, see you tomorrow.' She gave him a broad wink. 'Cheer up. Or I'll get Zo to sing to you, and she's got a tin ear!'

The house was silent when Kieran got home. Weirdly silent. The back of his neck prickled. Something was wrong. Badly wrong.

He took the stairs two at a time and knocked on Tess's door. No answer. Maybe she was asleep. He opened the door a crack. He could see Charlie in the cot, sleeping in his favourite position with his bottom stuck high in the air. But there was no sign of Tess.

If she wasn't in bed and she wasn't downstairs...then where was she? She would never have left her baby, Kieran knew.

He tried the bathroom door. Locked. 'Tess? Are you there?'

No reply.

Maybe she'd fallen asleep in the bath. Cried herself to sleep, after the way he'd behaved towards her. He knocked harder. 'Tess?'

Still no reply.

'I know you're angry with me, but just say something—anything—to let me know you're all right. Tess?'

Still no reply.

Was she that stubborn—or had something happened?

He didn't wait to go downstairs to get a knife and unpick the lock. He put his shoulder to the door and heaved until the lock gave way.

Tess was lying in the middle of the bathroom floor, a glass and an empty bottle of vodka next to her. And, more worryingly, a small box of pills. Paracetamol. And every capsule in the foil strip had been pushed through.

'No!' he yelled. 'Tess. Tess!' Paracetamol poisoning wouldn't make her drowsy or sleepy, he knew. Hopefully it was the vodka that had knocked her out—he hadn't noticed his sister drinking more than an occasional glass of wine in the evenings, so the spirits could have made her drunk to the point of unconsciousness.

He grabbed his mobile phone and punched in the number of the emergency services. 'I need an ambulance.' He gave his address, name and phone number. 'Suspected paracetamol poisoning—she's taken alcohol as well. I don't know how much or how long, but it's less than four hours.' Which meant there was a good chance of stopping any damage to her liver or kidneys. 'Please, just get someone here.' He double-checked the details then rang off.

'Don't you *dare* die on me, Tess Bailey,' he muttered as he checked her airway. Thank God, at least it was clear. She was breathing and her pulse was slow, but it *was* there.

'We're going to get through this. And this time I'm going to make damned sure you get proper help. For everything.' He kissed her cold, clammy forehead, then put her gently into the recovery position and checked the bathroom cabinet. Nothing else was missing—just the packet of paracetamol. So she'd taken a maximum of sixteen tablets.

Please, don't let there be another empty packet somewhere else.

As soon as the thought hit him, he rushed into Tess's bedroom and switched on the light. The room was a mess, but there was no sign of a box of paracetamol. The kitchen wastebin yielded nothing. Not willing to assume anything, he unlocked the back door and checked the dustbin. Nothing there either.

When the paramedics arrived, he gave them all Tess's details and as full a medical history as he could. 'I think she's taking antidepressants as well. I don't know what, so I'll bring her handbag—she keeps the tablets in there. These are the only paracetamol in the house and there aren't any other empty packets in the bin or anything. Assuming it was a new packet, she's taken sixteen tablets. There's nothing else missing. I don't know about the vodka—it was a house-warming present and I don't drink it, so I've no idea how much was in the bottle.' He took a deep breath. 'It might be worth trying activated charcoal—otherwise she needs methionine.' He shook his head. 'No. She's unconscious. Of course she's not going to be able to take it orally. She needs intravenous NAC to stop any renal or hepatic damage.'

'Medic, are you?' one of the paramedics asked.

'Obstetrician.'

'And she's your wife?'

'Sister,' he corrected. 'Just get her to ED. Please.'

While the paramedics took Tess out to the ambulance, Kieran wrapped Charlie in a blanket and grabbed Tess's handbag. There wasn't time to ring anyone else—right now, he had to get Tess to hospital as soon as possible.

He spent the next hour or so pacing the floor, holding Charlie and hoping that his nephew wasn't going to wake up and be frightened by the unfamiliar surroundings.

Tess could die. His baby sister could die. And it was all his fault.

Why, why, why hadn't he realised that things were this bad?

Stupid question. Because his mind had been elsewhere. Working through another part of his anatomy. He'd been concentrating more on his love-life than on his little sister. And she was paying the price.

At last one of the nurses came out of Resus.

'Mr Bailey?'

'Yes?'

'We've given her a gastric lavage.'

'So she's intubated?'

The nurse nodded. 'Her bloods aren't too bad. We're giving her intravenous NAC. Rick—the paramedic—said she might have been taking antidepressants.'

'I don't know what her GP gave her—she won't talk about it. But they're not in her handbag. And there wasn't any sign of overdosing on tricylics when I found her—no dilation of her pupils, no tachycardia.' Kieran bit his lip. 'I've got a nasty feeling she didn't even see her GP, let alone get a prescription. She's got postnatal depression and I've been nagging her too much about seeing someone about it.'

'She'll have to see someone about it now,' the nurse said wryly. 'We should be able to move her to an observation ward in another hour or so. You'll be able to see her then.'

Kieran nodded. 'I'd better ring our mum and tell her what's happened. Tess *is* going to be all right?'

'Fingers crossed.'

'Thanks for all your help.' He went into the reception area, found a payphone and prepared to ring his mother and explain what a total mess he'd made of looking after his baby sister.

Two hours later, Kieran was sitting next to Tess's bed in the general ward.

Her eyelids flickered and came open. 'Kieran?' she asked groggily, seeing him. 'Where am I?'

'London City General,' he said gently, taking her hand. 'How are you feeling?'

'Lousy. My stomach hurts.'

'It would do. They gave you a gastric lavage.'

'My head hurts, too.'

'That would be the after-effects of the vodka,' he said sagely.

Panic flickered across her face. 'Where's Charlie?'

'At home, with Mum. Who's not going to judge you, by the way. She's worried sick and loves you to bits. She's given me quite an ear-bashing, though. And deservedly so.'

A tear leaked down her face. 'I'm so sorry. I didn't mean this to happen.'

'You've got nothing to be sorry about, sweetheart. I'm the one who should be apologising. I was supposed to be looking after you and I made a rubbish job of it.' He paused. 'Why did you do it, Tess?'

Her eyes were huge as she looked at him. 'I just felt so lonely, so miserable. I couldn't face going to the doctor. I didn't want to go on drugs. But you kept nagging and nagging, and I felt as if you'd backed me into a corner. I didn't know what else to do. And then we had that fight and I just wanted everything to stop.'

'I'm so sorry, Tess. I shouldn't have pressured you.'

She gulped. 'I don't want to lose you.'

'Of course you're not going to lose me. I'm your big

brother.' He did his best to smile at her. 'You're stuck with me, squirt.'

'But I was in the way.'

Ice trickled down his spine. 'In the way of what?' he asked, trying to keep his tone as light as possible.

'I knocked your briefcase over. I'm sorry. I...' She shuddered. 'Anyway, all this stuff fell out. I put it back, but I saw this sticky note saying, "I love you." It was signed "J", with a heart. And you'd doodled "Jude" all over a bit of paper.' More tears slid down her face, unchecked. 'You were being so good to me, giving me a home and keeping Mum off my back, and all the time I was in the way. You couldn't even see your girlfriend because of me. And I'm such a mess you didn't even tell me you were seeing someone and it was serious.'

Kieran felt as if someone had just kicked him in the stomach. Hard. 'So tonight you did this...because of me and Jude?'

Tess was crying too hard to answer.

Kieran shifted to sit next to her on the bed. He held her close, stroking her hair. 'Oh, Tessikins. We never meant to hurt you. I didn't want to lie to you. Neither of us did. I didn't tell you about Jude because I was scared you'd think you were in the way and would run off to another grotty damp bedsit or something. I wanted to make sure you were all right before we told you about us.' He shuddered. 'This wasn't supposed to happen. None of this.'

She was still shaking with sobs, and he was aware that his own face was wet. 'Tess, I could have lost you—my baby sister.' And all because I'm just like my father. The pirate king. Taking what I want and to hell with anyone else—not even seeing how what I'm doing affects the people round me. 'I promise you, you've got nothing to worry about. Ever again.'

CHAPTER TWELVE

WHEN Judith's clock showed one in the morning and her phone was still obstinately silent, she gave up trying to read and turned off her bedside light. Kieran wasn't going to ring now. Maybe Charlie really wasn't well, and by the time Kieran had finished checking over his nephew and reassuring Tess, he'd probably thought it was too late to ring.

Judith yearned to ring him. Just to hear his voice. But she knew it wouldn't be fair to divide his loyalties. She'd see him in the morning. They could talk then.

But he didn't turn up for his shift. So something was definitely wrong. Kieran was on the same duty roster as her, and apart from his very first day he'd always been a good five or ten minutes early.

'Our revered consultant not in today?' Judith asked Daisy, hoping her voice sounded a lot more casual than she felt.

'Dunno. I haven't heard anything,' Daisy replied.

Judith didn't dare probe any more in case it started the hospital rumour mill. Maybe Charlie was sick. Maybe *Kieran* was sick.

At her break, she decided to take a chance and ring him at home. If Tess answered, Jude could always claim it was to do with work.

The phone rang one, twice, three times. Then the answering-machine recording started playing. It was halfway through when the receiver was picked up. 'Hello?'

A female voice. Not one she recognised. Judith's pulse

quickened. What was going on? 'Hello. Could I speak to Kieran Bailey, please?'

'I'm afraid he's not here.'

So where was he? Jude decided to stick to her original plan. 'It's Judith, from work. He didn't turn up this morning so I was just checking he was OK—there are some nasty bugs going round.' There weren't, but it was the only thing she could think of to say.

'He's OK.' There was a suspicious wobble in the woman's voice.

A nasty thought hit Jude. 'Charlie's not ill, is he?'

'Not Charlie.' There was a sound like a muffled sob. 'It's Tess. She…' There was a shuddering breath. 'My little girl took an overdose last night.'

'Oh, no.' Judith's stomach lurched. So *that* was why Tess hadn't answered the phone last night. She'd been sitting alone and miserable and desperate, and she'd taken the final step.

Then it sank in what the woman had said. *My little girl.* Tess's mother. Kieran's mother. Here, to pick up the pieces. If it wasn't already too late. What had Tess taken? Was she dead? Had Kieran found her in time? Had the overdose left her with irreversible damage to her liver, her kidneys, her heart, her lungs…? 'Is she—is Tess going to be all right, Mrs Bailey?' Judith asked shakily.

'I think so. She's still in hospital. Kieran's with her on the ward.'

Kieran. He must be feeling like hell. He'd had a fight with Tess before he'd gone out. No doubt he was blaming himself—for not seeing how low Tess was, for rowing with her, for going out and leaving her on her own.

'I'm so sorry. Look, if there's anything I can do…' Anything. Though what she really wanted was to rush to Kieran's side. To comfort him, hold him, reassure him that it wasn't his fault, that his little sister would be OK and everything would work out just fine.

'Who is it again?'

'Judith Powell. I'm Kieran's…' She stopped herself saying 'girlfriend' just in time. 'Registrar.'

'I'll tell him you called.'

'Is it all right if I go to see Tess and take her some flowers?' Something pretty and cheerful to brighten up her surroundings.

'If you want to. She's on the women's general ward.'

'Thank you.'

Judith skipped lunch and went straight to the hospital shop to buy flowers. But when she got to the women's general ward, the sister informed her that Tess already had the maximum number of visitors—more than that, actually, but they were making allowances for the baby.

Kieran, his mother and Charlie, Judith guessed. And she wasn't family. Didn't have any status, really. She was Kieran's secret girlfriend. Something squeezed at her heart. She shouldn't be here. It wasn't her place to intrude.

But how she wanted to be side by side with Kieran, holding his hand. Getting to know Tess, too, letting her know that she had a friend who'd be there for her, who'd listen without judging.

Though it would look strange, coming from someone who was supposed to be merely a colleague. If she insisted on going in, she'd make things worse for Kieran. Step up the pressure. And he already had enough to deal with. She had to put him first—no matter how sad or angry or miserable or frustrated she felt, this wasn't the time or the place to do anything about it.

'Could I, um, leave these for Tess?' she asked, holding the flowers she'd bought.

'Of course. Who shall I say they're from?'

'Judith Powell—I work with her brother. Maybe I can pop back later and see how she is?'

'Sure.'

Though by the time Judith's shift was over, she felt drained—and too apprehensive to go back to the general ward. If Kieran had wanted her to be there, he'd have got a message to her somehow—even if it was only an acknowledgement of the flowers.

His silence told her the one thing she didn't want to face: she didn't belong.

At eight o'clock that evening, when Kieran still hadn't phoned her, Judith started really worrying. Was Tess's condition more serious than the sister had let on? What *had* Tess taken? Was it something that could mean days before the final effects were known?

And was Kieran all right? If he'd been at Tess's bedside since the moment he'd found her, he couldn't have had much sleep, apart from dozing in the visitor's chair. He probably hadn't eaten anything either—maybe a sandwich from the canteen's trolley service, but not enough to keep his strength up. Guilt dragged at her. She should be doing something positive, something to help, not sitting here and feeling sorry for herself. She dialled the hospital's number and asked to be put through to the ward where Tess was.

'Hello, Women's General, Staff Nurse speaking.'

'Hello. I wondered if you could tell me how Tess Bailey is, please?'

'Are you a relative?'

There had been enough lies. 'No,' Judith said.

'She's comfortable.'

Judith had said the same thing too many times to enquirers at Maternity to be happy with the response. 'Comfortable' could mean just about anything. 'Thank you,' she said quietly, and hung up.

She had to find out somehow. She could call Kieran, but

he was probably at the hospital. She didn't really want to leave a message on his answering-machine, and his mobile phone would be switched off while he was on the ward. Besides, she didn't want to put any extra pressure on him. He'd be worried sick about his sister and he didn't need his girlfriend whining for attention.

That left her with one option.

Waiting. Until he was ready to tell her.

On Friday, Kieran was back at work. Judith restrained herself from rushing in to ask what was going on, but eventually armed herself with a couple of files and rapped on his door. 'Morning. Got a moment?'

'Of course.'

His voice was cool, but she didn't let it faze her. She closed the door behind her and dropped all pretence of her visit being about work. 'How's Tess?'

'She'll live. No thanks to us.'

She frowned. 'What?'

'She tried to kill herself because of *us*.'

'Oh, God, no.' She dropped the files on his desk, moved to stand next to him and slid her arms round his shoulders. 'I'm so sorry.'

He shrugged her away. 'Just leave it, Jude.'

'I can't. What happened?'

'I think my mother's already told you,' he said shortly.

She sighed. 'OK, so maybe I shouldn't have called you at home. But I was worried about you when you didn't turn up at work yesterday.'

'I left a message that there was a family problem and I'd be in today.'

'No one told me.' Though why should they? She was only his registrar.

His eyes were dark and his face was grim. She could imagine the guilt that was eating him up inside. 'Kieran, it's not your fault that Tess—'

'Leave it,' he said again.

'But it's not—' she began.

'Judith, even if you're not busy, I am.'

At the look of disgust on his face, she recoiled as if he'd slapped her. Surely she was the one person he knew he could always talk to? But he'd made it clear that he didn't want to talk.

And he also didn't want *her* anywhere near him.

She picked up her files and left his office without another word. Outwardly, she was a competent obstetric registrar. Inwardly, she felt as if someone had put her down in the middle of a frozen landscape, a place where everything looked the same as far as the eye could see, and there were no signs to show her the way back home. Lost and alone, with nowhere to go. She'd been so sure that Kieran loved her, just as she loved him. That they could face anything, as long as they were together.

But she'd been wrong. So wrong. It hurt so much that her emotions had gone into deep freeze. Kieran didn't want comfort—not from her, at any rate. He'd shut himself away behind a wall that was so high and so deep she didn't even know where to start trying to find a way through it.

And even if she did, there were no guarantees that he'd let her get close.

He was curt with her for the rest of the day, even when they ended up working on an emergency case of a prolapsed cord, where the baby's umbilical cord was particularly long and part of it had passed through the entrance to the mother's uterus. If the cord was pressed between the baby's head and the mother's body, the blood flow through the cord would be restricted, so the baby wouldn't get enough oxygen and would become distressed—and might even die.

As soon as Judith realised what was happening, she sent Daisy to fetch Kieran and bleep for an anaesthetist for an emergency section—the baby's head wasn't far down enough in Maxine's pelvis for her to risk doing a forceps delivery. She got Maxine to kneel and put her head down and push her bottom in the air to slow things down, then pushed the baby's head back up during contractions to make sure there wasn't any extra pressure on the cord.

The little girl was born safely but Kieran barely acknowledged the way Judith had managed the situation, saving the baby's life. He simply stalked off and shut himself in his office again.

That night, Judith rang his mobile but it was switched off. It stayed switched off for the whole of the weekend—while he was off duty—and although Judith rushed home after her shifts, the red light on her answering-machine stayed unlit. And every time she checked the number of the last person who'd called her, it was never his.

She dialled Zoe's number three times on the Saturday, but hung up before the call was connected. It was the weekend. Zoe was barely back from honeymoon. How could Jude be selfish enough to drag her best friend away from her new husband, just to whine about how impossible Kieran was being?

She knew she could call her other best friend—Holly was only next door—but she also knew that Holly was working nights. Weekend nights were always the busiest in the emergency department, so what Holly needed after her shift was sleep, not coffee and trying to hide her yawns as she listened to Jude.

Particularly as she hadn't told either of them what was really going on.

She'd just have to stop being silly and concentrate on what she was supposed to be doing. Working as a registrar in the maternity department of a busy London hospital. And Kieran would calm down over the weekend and start talking to her…wouldn't he? Just give it forty-eight hours.

By the time Judith's two days off began on Monday morning, she realised that Kieran wasn't going to ring her. So Friday in his office hadn't been just shock, hadn't been a reaction that he'd get over. He wasn't going to call her. Wasn't going to let her comfort him. Because he associated her with the guilt he felt about what Tess had done, and that guilt was too strong for any other emotion to overcome it.

Guilt that she felt, too. He had a point. If they hadn't kept their relationship from Tess, she wouldn't have reacted so badly when she'd found out.

Knowing that Kieran was at work so it would be safe to visit Tess, Judith bought an armful of flowers and headed for London City General.

'I understand if you don't want to see me,' she said quietly when she walked into Tess's cubicle, 'but I wanted to apologise in person. And to bring you these—not that they can even begin to make up for anything.' She handed Tess the bouquet of flowers.

'Thank you. They're lovely,' Tess said, smiling at her.

'I swear, I never meant to hurt you, Tess. Neither of us did.'

'Kee's already told me.' Tess bit her lip. 'And I feel so stupid now.'

'No. You were unhappy. Ill. And we should have seen that instead of being wrapped up in each other.' Judith handed her a small gold box. 'These are for you, too. The best pick-me-up I know.'

Tess looked inside. 'Chocolates?'

'Better than chocolate,' Judith promised. 'It's gianduja. I should warn you, they, um, disappear rather quickly.'

'You came to see me on your day off?'

Judith nodded. 'It's the least I can do, considering it's my fault you're in here.'

'You didn't exactly pour the vodka into the glass for me. Or hand me the paracetamol,' Tess said wryly.

'But I didn't ring you when I said I would to invite you to join me, Zoe and Holly for a pizza.'

Tess shrugged. 'It's OK. I thought you were just being polite.'

'No. I did mean it. I just…' She'd just spent all her time thinking about Tess's brother. Selfish in the extreme. Judith bit her lip. 'How's Charlie?'

'Being spoiled rotten by my mum.'

'Sorry, I should have thought to bring him something, too.'

Tess shook her head. 'No need. But thanks anyway.'

'I'll, um, let you get some rest. Maybe I can come and see you again?'

'I'd like that,' Tess said.

Though Judith had a feeling that Kieran most definitely wouldn't.

He didn't ring her during her two days off. And on Wednesday, when she started the late shift, he was very cool towards her.

By the mid-afternoon break, she'd had enough. She banged on his office door and, without waiting for him to invite her in, marched in, closed the door behind her and leaned on it.

'What?' he asked, looking up and scowling.

'You know what, Kieran. You're freezing me out.'

'No, I'm not.'

'You're barely even civil to me on the ward. If you don't want people talking about you, you're going the wrong way about it.'

'Right now, I couldn't care less what anyone thinks.'

Including me? Judith asked silently. 'I saw Tess on Monday.'

'I know.'

She sighed. 'Kieran, I know you're worried about your sister and I'm trying to be patient, really I am, but you're driving me crazy. I hate it that you're shutting me out. Talk to me. I'm here for you and I'm not going to spread gossip. You know that.'

He said nothing.

If she'd had anything to throw at him, she would have lobbed it straight at his head—out of sheer frustration. Why did he have to be so stubborn and convinced that he could go it alone? 'What about us?' she asked.

His face was impassive and she couldn't tell what he was thinking. His tone didn't give much away either when he said quietly, 'There is no us. Not any more.'

'What?' She could hardly take in what she'd just heard. Kieran was dumping her? But...he'd said he loved her. He'd said words to her that she knew he'd never said to anyone else. He loved her. She loved him. They both knew it. It was *right* between them. So why was he ending it?

Her head was spinning. Maybe she was in some weird parallel world. Maybe this was the most realistic nightmare she'd ever had—maybe she'd wake up and she'd be at home and the duvet would be on the floor and she'd be so relieved that her muscles wouldn't work enough to let her pull the covers back over her.

But if it was a nightmare, why had his voice been so clear?

'Why?' she whispered.

His mouth thinned. 'You know why. My sister tried to kill herself because of us.'

'No. Tess tried to kill herself because she'd hit rock bottom.'

'And I didn't see how bad it was—because I wasn't paying attention.'

Because he'd been thinking about her. It was written all over his face.

So it was her fault? He was blaming *her*? No. That wasn't fair. What had happened to Tess was awful, but it was nobody's fault. 'You're using Tess as an excuse. The real reason you don't want to be with me is because you're too screwed up to trust anyone or be in a relationship with anybody.'

Bile rose in her stomach as she realised she'd been right about him from the start. She'd picked another bad guy. If Kieran really loved her, he wouldn't end it. He wouldn't let her go. He'd let her comfort him.

But he didn't make a single move to stop her when she walked away. He didn't ring her later that night. And Judith realised at three o'clock next morning that Kieran wasn't ever going to call. He simply didn't care that her heart was breaking.

Work was awful for the next couple of weeks. Going in to the ward and pretending that she was her usual cheery self, when inside she wanted to howl, was the hardest thing Judith had ever done. But she loved it at London City General and she had no intention of moving hospitals just because she'd split up with Kieran. Besides, nobody at work had any idea of their relationship, so it wasn't as if she was going to have to face all the misplaced sympathy. She'd get through it all just fine. And eventually she'd be able to walk into the ward without all her senses going onto red alert. She wouldn't keep missing him. Keep wanting him.

What she didn't bargain for were her best friends. One evening when she answered the door, Zoe and Holly virtually frogmarched her into her kitchen.

'What?' she asked. 'Aren't you two supposed to be at Giovanni's?'

'With you,' Holly said. 'Except you called off. For the second time in a row. And you haven't been seen anywhere near the local take-aways. I don't believe you've suddenly decided that you like cooking, so clearly you're not eating properly.'

'And if you won't come to Giovanni's, Giovanni's will come to you,' Zoe informed her, waving two carrier bags at her.

Judith frowned. 'Giovanni's doesn't do take-aways.'

'They do when Holls puts her scary face on,' Zoe said with a grin.

Virtually before Judith had time to blink, Holly had laid the table, Zoe had put the pizza, garlic bread and salad on plates, and the pair of them had shoved her into a chair and put a glass of wine in her hand.

'Eat now, talk later,' Zoe said.

'There's nothing to tell,' Judith lied.

'We've known you too long for you to get away with that,' Holly warned. 'You've been too quiet when we've met you for lunch, too. So you're going to tell us everything, after you've had some of Giovanni's best.'

Judith sighed. 'I give in.'

When Judith had cleared her plate and finished a portion of Giovanni's special cheesecake, with ice cream on the side, Zoe put a jug of coffee before them, together with the remains of a box of gianduja from Jude's fridge.

'So. Talk,' Zoe said.

'There's nothing wrong.'

'Jude, I live next to you,' Holly said.

Judith frowned. 'And?'

'And you've spent the last couple of weeks doing nothing but playing the piano.'

She winced. 'Sorry. I didn't realise I was being so noisy. Oh, God. I didn't wake you when you were on nights, did I?'

'Don't be silly. You're not being a noisy neighbour and your music's fabulous. But the stuff you've been playing is the stuff of heartbreak,' Holly said.

'It's Kieran, isn't it?' Zoe asked.

Judith lifted her chin. She hadn't even told her best friends about him. 'What makes you think that?'

'The fact that your face lit up every time he walked into the room,' Zoe said. 'The fact that you were singing to him—and don't deny it. Brad said he noticed it too.'

Judith groaned. 'Oh, hell. Is everybody talking about it?'

'No. We just know you better than everyone else,' Holly said. 'Plus, when someone tries to look inconspicuous when they're leaving your neighbour's house at a strange time of night…'

Judith put her head in her hands. 'Oh, no. I didn't even think about that. You should have gone into law, Holls. You'd scare any criminal into confessing everything.'

'We're only nagging because we love you,' Zoe said, gently pulling Judith's hands away from her face. 'What went wrong?'

Judith told them about Tess. About how Kieran had given up on their relationship at its first serious test.

'And you're still in love with him?' Holly asked.

'But he doesn't love me.' Judith shrugged. 'I'm a big girl. I'll get over it. Pass me some gianduja.'

'Jude, maybe you ought to give it another go. Talk to him,' Zoe counselled.

'I've already tried that. He's not interested. And I'm not going to make him despise me by being pathetic and whining and refusing to admit that it's over.' Judith unwrapped another piece of gianduja. 'I'll be fine.'

Though her words had a hollow ring to them.

Judith threw all her energies into work. And when Margot asked her to have a chat with one of the new mums, who was complaining of tenderness in her left leg, Judith didn't even need to look anything up in her handbook.

'Hi, Kerry. How's little Ned?'

'He's doing fine, thanks,' Kerry said with a smile.

'Gorgeous boy. You're going to be a heartbreaker,' Judith said, stroking the baby's cheek. 'Kerry, Margot says your leg feels a bit funny. Can I take a look?'

'Sure.' Kerry shifted so that Judith could examine her left leg. 'I feel a bit silly, making a fuss.'

'Not at all.' Kerry's leg felt slightly hot to the touch and looked slightly puffy. 'Does it hurt here?' Judith asked.

'It's a bit tender. Nothing like giving birth, of course.'

'But you still shouldn't have to put up with it. Kerry, I'm going to send you for an ultrasound scan just to check your leg out—it's possible that there's a blood clot there.'

'You mean, like some people get when they've been on a plane?'

Judith nodded. 'We know about it so it shouldn't be a problem.' Kerry was at a higher risk of VTE, as she was thirty-seven, overweight and hadn't been on her feet much since the birth. 'I'm going to give you some heparin just to help thin your blood a little bit—what we call anticoagulant therapy—and if the scan confirms it, I'll be able to do something more.'

Venous thromboembolism or VTE—a blood clot in a vein—could occur at any stage of pregnancy, but the highest risk was in the couple of days after the birth. If Judith left the suspected VTE without doing anything about it, the clot could go into the lungs. If it did this and became a pulmonary embolism, it could cause breathing problems, collapse and even death.

'Before I start you on the heparin, I'm going to do some blood tests so I know what's going on.' She took a sample. 'Margot, can you get this off to the lab for Us and Es, full blood count, coag screen, thrombophilia screen and LFTs?' Testing the urea, electrolytes and liver function would show if there were any problems with Kerry's lungs or liver, when it would be dangerous to give her anticoagulants.

'What happens if the scan shows a clot?'

'We'll give you heparin for a few weeks and it should disperse the clot,' Judith explained. 'We'll check you at the end of the course to see how things are going and if you need to continue with the treatment. It's also a good idea for you to wear an elastic compression stocking on your left leg—I'm afraid that'll be for quite a lot longer, maybe as long as two years.'

'Two years?'

'Wear trousers all the time,' Judith advised with a smile. 'Better to commit a few fashion sins than take risks with your health.'

Kerry nodded.

'I'll be back to see you when you've had your scan and your blood test results are back,' Judith promised.

Her diagnosis turned out to be spot on, so she arranged a loading dose of heparin and a continuous IV infusion, with daily blood tests and the lab results to come straight to her.

That was one thing Kieran had done for her, she thought as she changed at the end of her shift. Nowadays she didn't panic—she just got on with her job. He'd given her self-confidence. Professionally.

Personally, it was another matter. Without even realising it, she began singing, 'I'll never fall in love again'.

'You OK, Jude?' Louise asked, coming in.

'I'm fine, Lulu.'

'Bit of a mournful song, isn't it?'

Judith shrugged. 'I'm just practising a new set for the fundraisers. Heartbreakers always bring in more donations.'

'Now you're talking. We could do with another colour Doppler,' Louise said with a smile.

*　　*　　*

In the corridor outside, Kieran turned away as soon as Judith stopped singing. She could have been singing for him—because he was never going to fall in love again. Judith was his one and only. But after what had happened, it just wasn't possible for them to be together. He'd only end up hurting her—just like he'd hurt Tess—because he was so damned selfish. Just like his father.

So he was never, ever going to fall in love again.

CHAPTER THIRTEEN

KIERAN sniffed as he walked indoors. Was it his imagination, or could he smell food? Proper food?

'I'm home,' he called.

'Hiya.' To his surprise, Tess emerged from the kitchen. 'I hope you're hungry.'

'Starving.'

'It's only chicken breasts, salad and new potatoes—it's not really up to your standard,' she added diffidently.

He grinned. 'Correction. It's champagne standard—because it looks as if I've got my baby sister back!' He picked her up and whirled her round.

'Put me down!' Tess laughed, and shrugged as he set her back on her feet. 'Well, it was about time I pulled myself together.'

'Tess, you were clinically depressed. It's not something you can sort on your own,' he reminded her. 'Want a hand with anything?'

'No. Just sit and enjoy. Charlie's zonked—must have been all that walking he did at Tots this afternoon. He's still holding my fingers, but he's really getting there.'

This was the Tess Kieran was used to. Full of energy, doing things, socialising—it wouldn't surprise him if she'd already agreed to host a coffee-morning for the toddler group she'd started attending. In the month that she'd been seeing a counsellor about her depression and started medication, she'd gone back to her old self. She'd been talking about maybe going back to college part time and finishing her art course, or seeing if she could find herself a part-time job in an ad agency or design studio. Charlie had blossomed, too, and was at the stage of cruising the furniture and toddling a few steps if he had a finger to hold onto.

Life was moving on.

So why was he still yearning for something he couldn't have?

But he'd already been selfish enough. He wasn't going to wallow in his misery and knock Tess back again now. 'That was gorgeous,' Kieran pronounced when he'd finished his meal. 'What did you put in the marinade?'

'Cajun spices and lime juice. Cassie at Tots suggested it to me.' Tess propped her elbows on the dining room table. 'Kee, you look as bad as I used to feel.'

'I'm fine,' he said lightly.

'You look as if you haven't slept properly for weeks.'

'We're busy at work.'

Tess narrowed her eyes. 'You promised you weren't going to lie to me again. It's Jude, isn't it? Did she dump you because your sister's a basket case?' Her lips thinned. 'If she did, just forget her—because she's not worth it.'

'Jude isn't like that.'

'If she dumped you then, yes, she is.'

He shook his head. 'I was the one who ended it.'

'What? You idiot!' She stared at him. 'Why?'

'Long story.'

'I'm not going anywhere.'

He didn't want to talk about it.

Tess plonked a mug of coffee in front of him. 'You're not going anywhere either until you tell me. You made me promise to tell you if I feel bad again. The same goes for you. That's what family's for, isn't it?'

Kieran gave in, and told her what he'd explained to Judith about his father.

When he'd finished, Tess gave him a hug. 'Oh, Kee. I'm

sorry. I had no idea. Does Mum know?' She slapped her forehead. 'Duh! I mean, about the bits after he left her.'

'Not all of it, no. And I wouldn't want her to be with him still anyway—Martyn's perfect for her and they love each other to bits.' He sighed. 'But the more I think about it, the more I realise I'm just like my father.'

Tess scoffed. 'Don't be so stupid. If you were, you'd have left me to die and put Charlie in a home—oh, and probably cheated on Jude with twenty other women.'

He pulled a face. 'That's a bit extreme.'

'Exactly. And you're being extreme now. Look, you're meant to be the clever one. You went to Cambridge, not me.'

Guilt flashed through him. 'Tess, I hope you haven't been feeling that you have to compete with me.'

'No, of course I haven't.' She grinned. 'Nobody in their right mind wants to be a geek.'

He rolled his eyes at her. 'I'm not a geek.'

'Yes, you are.' Tess put her hands on her hips. 'Otherwise you'd realize that whatever you think, you are *not* like your dad. You're not a sad, selfish old git who needs to grow up. You love Jude, and she loves you. So why don't you stop being so stupid and get back together?'

Kieran shook his head. 'I wasn't very nice to her. She'll never forgive me.'

'How do you know unless you give her the chance?'

'Just leave it, Tess.'

She shrugged. 'There's no point in nagging you because you won't listen.'

'That's a bit rich, coming from you!'

She grinned. 'Yeah. I think you've got more in common with me than with your dad. Kee, are you busy on Friday night? I was thinking, maybe we could go out.'

What? She actually wanted to go out somewhere?

She seemed oblivious to his surprise. 'I'll ask Rosemary

to babysit. She adores Charlie and he really likes her. We'll go out for a pizza, then to a club.'

Kieran groaned. 'Please. I'm too old for clubbing.'

'You're thirty-two, not sixty-two. Act your age.' She gave him a calculating look. 'If you're worried about all your grey hairs, don't. I'll get some dye from the chemist tomorrow so I can cover them for you, then nobody will notice.'

'I do not have grey hairs.' Did he?

She chucked. 'Ha, had you going there! Kee, it'll do us both good to get out and let our hair down.'

She was right. He knew that.

'Actually, I could get myself a new outfit for Friday. Tell you what, I'll meet you after work at Giovanni's.'

His heart contracted. Giovanni's? It was one of Jude's haunts. She might be there. Then again, so what if she was? It was over between them. He had to move on. Even if it was killing him.

Tess was still talking. 'You can take your stuff to work and get changed after your shift. Wear your silk shirt, the one with all the blues and purples—I like you in that.'

'Hang on, *I'm* supposed to be the bossy one.'

'Nope. I'm back. Get used to it.' Tess winked at him. 'I'll book the table tomorrow. You can meet me there on Friday when you've finished work. No worries if you're held up—I'll hit the sparkling mineral water. I might live really dangerously and have a slice of lime in it.'

'Sounds as if I'm in your hands, sis,' he said, resigned—though it was good to have his bubbly, bouncy kid sister back again.

If only he could have Jude, too.

But it wasn't going to happen, and there was no point in dreaming.

*   *   *

The following morning, Judith's phone rang.

'Maternity, Judith Powell speaking.'

'Hiya, Jude. It's Tess.'

Judith froze. Kieran's sister was ringing her? 'How are you?' she asked carefully.

'Lots better, thanks. How about you?'

'Fine,' Judith lied. Part of her wanted to ask about Kieran, to find out how he *really* was underneath the ice-cold person he'd become on the ward, but she stopped herself. She didn't want Tess telling him she'd asked—or Kieran thinking she was desperate. Even if she *was* desperate.

'Listen, about that pizza you suggested—are you still up for it? I could do with a girly night out,' Tess said.

Judith was slightly taken aback. 'When?'

'Friday night.'

'I don't think Zoe can make it—she's out somewhere with Brad, and I know Holly's on duty.'

'That's a shame, but we can still have fun, just the two of us. I'll get a table—Giovanni's does good food, I think you said?'

'The best. OK, I'd love to. What about a babysitter—or do you want to bring Charlie with you?'

'No worries. I've got a babysitter very close by,' Tess said.

Judith assumed she meant Kieran. 'Just you and me, then.'

'We can go clubbing afterwards.'

And dance away her heartache. 'I'm up for that.'

'Good. Meet me there. I'll book the table in your name. If one of us is late, the other'll just have to eat all the breadsticks. Wear slinky stuff—oh, and bring your spare lippy!'

'You're on.'

Judith was smiling by the time she put the phone down. Tess sounded so much better. If only Kieran… But there was no point in kidding herself. It wasn't going to happen. They were colleagues only now, sticking to polite neutrality whenever they couldn't actively avoid each other.

On Friday evening, Judith walked into Giovanni's. 'Hi. I've got a table booked—Judith Powell?'

'This way,' the waiter said.

Her smile faded when she saw who was already sitting at the table next to hers. Kieran. At a table for two. Her stomach clenched. He was going on a date. With another woman. And she would have to sit there and pretend it didn't matter. For Tess's sake, she'd have to smile and laugh through the whole evening.

Right now, she wanted to beat her fists on the table and howl. It hadn't taken him long to find someone else.

If only it could still have been her.

Oh, no. He'd known there was a chance she'd be here— but why did she have to sit at the table right next to his? Kieran nodded politely at Judith, but inside he was raging. He'd change places with Tess once she arrived so he didn't have to watch Jude and her date snuggling up together. On the other hand, changing places would mean that he'd be able to overhear the conversation between Jude and her new man. He wasn't sure he could handle that either.

Why had she had to move on right here, right now?

He tried to concentrate on the menu, but he was too aware of Jude. Of the vanilla scent of her perfume. And she looked fabulous. Hair loose, slinky black dress, just enough make-up to accentuate her beauty, and high heels.

And in his mind he could still see every inch of her long, long legs. Remember how they'd felt wrapped round his waist. Remember…

He couldn't handle this. As soon as Tess arrived, he'd make some excuse and they could go somewhere else.

Just then his mobile phone beeped.

He sighed. It was probably Tess, telling him that she was running just a little bit behind schedule.

He flicked into the 'messages' screen. As he'd expected, the text was from his little sister. So how late was she going to be?

Small prob. Treble-booked. Y dont u 2 eat 2gether?

Treble-booked? Then who were the other two? Eat together…did she mean with *Jude*?

He looked up to find Judith staring at him, looking as shocked as he felt.

'Does your text say the same as mine?' she asked.

He handed his phone to her. She read the screen and groaned. 'Yes.'

'She's set us up,' he said in disbelief. Then hope began to creep into his veins. 'So you weren't on a date?'

She shook her head. 'And you?'

'No.'

Both mobile phones bleeped again. In unison, they read Tess's second text.

Told staff u r *not* 2 leave till u talked. Properly.

'My little sister's got bossy tendencies,' he said wryly.

'It runs in the family,' Judith muttered.

He nodded to her table. 'May I join you?'

She shrugged. 'Suit yourself.'

He came to sit opposite her and sighed. 'Jude, I'm sorry. I know I hurt you.'

'Yes. You did.'

'If it makes you feel any better, I'm hurting, too,' he said softly.

Her mouth tightened. 'You didn't even tell me that Tess was in hospital. I found out from your mum.'

'I'm sorry. I was upset. Mixed up. Guilty. She told me she did it so she wouldn't be in our way.'

'And now she's trying to get us back together.'

Help. He needed help. To make sure he said the right

thing, didn't make things even worse. As the silence length-ened between them, Kieran's pulse quickened with panic. 'Jude, I don't know what to say. I don't know how to make it right.'

'I don't think you can,' she said quietly. 'You made it perfectly clear that it's over between us.'

But he didn't want it to be over. He was sitting close enough to touch her. All he had to do was reach out and touch her. Tell her the truth. Tell her he'd been in hell since the day he'd told her they were through.

'I've missed you,' he said. 'Pushing you away was the most stupid thing I've ever done.'

Her eyes said it all for her. *But you still did it.*

'Tess nearly died because I was so self-absorbed. So I had to start thinking about what was best for other people, not just what I wanted. I warned you I had a major per-sonality flaw. So it would be better for you if I stayed away from you.'

She said nothing.

'I know I hurt you and I hate myself for that—but I really had your best interests at heart.'

'Why didn't you ask me what I wanted?'

He frowned. 'How do you mean?'

'You decided what was best for me. But you didn't credit me with enough sense to make my own decision. You didn't ask me what I wanted.'

Past tense, he noted. 'What did you want?'

'To comfort you. To be there with you. To help you and Tess get through it. Yes, I know I was the one who sug-gested keeping it quiet. But I'm not perfect. I got it wrong.'

That made two of them.

His mouth was so dry, he could barely force the words out. 'And what do you want now?'

She took a deep, shuddering breath, but she didn't say anything.

'I heard you singing. On the ward, that is—I couldn't face coming to the last fundraiser, and knowing that you were out of reach. But you were singing "I'll never fall in love again".' He reached out and took her hand. 'That's how I feel. I'll never fall in love again. Because even though I've told myself I'm wrong for you, that I'm going to make a mess of your life, I'm still in love with you. I wake every morning and it hurts like hell that you're not beside me. I read textbooks every night until I can't see straight, because if I don't I'll start thinking about you and missing you. I can't even listen to the radio any more because it makes me remember you singing to me. Nobody else is ever going to make me feel the way you do.' His fingers tightened round hers. 'Will you give me another chance, Jude?'

'And what happens the next time a crisis hits you? Will you push me away again?'

He wanted to say no—but he owed her the truth. 'I don't know. I'll try not to.'

'Kieran, there's still too much unresolved stuff going on in your head. You need to see your father and make your peace with him.'

'How? I don't even know where he is.'

'Until you've proved to yourself that you're not the same, there's always going to be that doubt in your mind. It's going to come between us, and the cracks are going to get a little bit bigger every day.' She shook her head. 'I'm not prepared to do that, Kieran. I don't want to lose the man I love, little by little, because of something that isn't even true.'

She still loved him?

Her eyes filled with tears. 'But you have to see it for yourself. Until you do, there's no point in getting back together. Because we're only going to hurt each other.'

'I love you, Jude. Believe me.'

'I do. But until you believe in yourself,' she said quietly, 'it's not going to work.' She pushed her chair back and stood up. 'I'm going home now. On my own.'

'What about us?'

'Call me when…' Her voice wobbled. 'Call me when you've sorted out who you really are.'

He wanted to go after her. To carry her home. To kiss her until she promised to give him another chance. But that was the pirate king talking. And he knew deep down that she was right. If he didn't trust himself, he wouldn't let her trust him either, and the love she felt for him would fade into bitterness.

He owed it to her to face his demons. Now.

He switched his mobile phone back on. 'Hi, Mum.' He wanted to ask her straight away, but that was the pirate king again. He had to take it slower. So he chatted to her for a few minutes before asking. 'Just on the off chance, are you still in touch with the Galloways?' His father's family.

'You want your dad's number.'

It was a statement, not a question. How did she know?

Before he even asked her, he heard her chuckle wryly. 'Tess told me.'

He groaned. 'She wasn't supposed to.'

'No more secrets, remember? She didn't tell me everything, Kee, just that you were convinced you're like your father.' She sighed. 'You're not, but the only way you're going to prove it to yourself is to see him.'

Exactly what Jude had said. They had a point. But he couldn't stop the fear rising. What if he saw his father and they *were* alike?

'Got a pen?'

'Sure.' He scribbled down the number she gave him.

'I'm here if you need to talk, love,' she said softly. 'I

know you're a grown man, but I'm still your mother. Never forget that.'

'I won't.'

'Love you, Kee.'

'I...' He swallowed hard. He was *not* going to give up on this at the first hurdle. He was going to say the words he should have said many, many times before. 'I love you, too, Mum.'

Kieran spent the next hour walking and wondering. They hadn't spoken for years. Why would Tom Galloway even want to talk to his son now?

There was only one way to find out. He dialled the number. It was a Friday night so the chances were Tom was out. He might have to wait until tomorrow.

'Hello?'

Adrenalin pumped through Kieran. 'Can I speak to Tom Galloway?' he asked.

'Speaking.'

'It's Kieran.'

There was a long, long silence, and for a moment Kieran wondered if his father had hung up. 'My son?'

'Yes. I, um, wondered if we could meet for a drink some time.'

'Why?'

How could he possibly say, So I can prove to myself I'm not the heartless bastard you are?

'It's been a long time,' Tom said, when it was clear that Kieran wasn't going to answer his question.

'Yes.'

'It'd be good to see you. When?'

Right now. 'How about tomorrow night?'

'Sure. Do you know the White Horse? It's near Wood Lane station. They sell decent beer.'

'OK. Seven o'clock?' Kieran asked.

'Seven's fine.'

'How will I...how will we recognise each other?' Kieran asked. 'Should I...I dunno, carry a copy of the *Financial Times* or something?'

'No need. I'll know you,' Tom said softly.

CHAPTER FOURTEEN

KIERAN had to force himself to concentrate at work the next day. When his shift was over, he had to face an interrogation and a clothes inspection from Tess, followed by a phone call from their mother just to check that he was all right about meeting his father, and he was nearly late leaving the house.

He wouldn't have minded so much if Jude had called him. He'd nearly dialled her number a dozen times that day, to tell her what was going on. But he'd always hung up before he was halfway through her number. She'd made it clear. *Call me when you've sorted out who you really are.*

Tonight, he promised silently. I'll sort it out tonight.

The trains were running perfectly and he walked into the White Horse at precisely five minutes to seven. Tom was bound to be late—he always had been when he'd picked Kieran up from his mother's. He'd be wearing a trendy shirt with an open neck showing too much gold jewellery, and he'd be chatting up the barmaid. Or anyone else in a skirt who happened to catch his eye, just as he had when Kieran had been small. His hair would definitely be dyed—no way would Tom Galloway admit to being over thirty, despite having a son who was thirty-two—and he'd probably already visited a few other pubs on his way to the White Horse.

Kieran scanned the bar. He couldn't see anybody remotely like he was expecting.

Then the tall, grey-haired man in the corner stood up and came towards him. 'Kieran?'

'Yes.' *This* was his father? But…the man was dressed perfectly normally, in a nondescript shirt and a pair of casual trousers. Normal shoes, not trendy loafers. Short grey hair, thinning slightly.

He looked like anybody else's father.

Not the man that Kieran remembered.

'Let me buy you a drink,' Tom said, seemingly oblivious to the shock rippling through Kieran.

'Um, do you recommend anything?' What did he call him? Dad? Tom? Kieran couldn't remember what he'd decided last night. Nothing seemed to fit, right now, so he took refuge in not actually calling his father anything at all.

'Sure.'

Kieran couldn't help watching his father with the barmaid. She looked a good ten years younger than Kieran—technically, that would make her young enough to be his father's granddaughter. But Tom didn't flirt with her, as Kieran had half expected. He simply ordered two pints, was pleasant to the girl without leering at her, and then handed Kieran a glass.

'Thank you.'

'Shall we…?'

Kieran followed Tom to the quiet table in the corner.

'You've changed,' he said.

Tom nodded. 'I've grown up, son. Something I should have done years ago.' He took a sip of his beer. 'I should have apologised to you years ago, too.'

Kieran shook his head, not knowing what to say.

'So what are you doing now? Still a doctor?'

'Obstetrician,' Kieran said. 'I'm at London City General. I, um, got a consultant's post this year.'

'You always were clever.' Tom smiled ruefully. 'I could never really follow you. I suppose that's why I tried to—well, why I did what I did last time I saw you. To prove that your old man could do just as well as you, even without an education. Except I couldn't. I just made us both look a fool.' He sighed. 'You've no idea how much I've regretted it since. Are you married now?'

'No.'

'Anyone special?'

'Could be.'

Tom raised an eyebrow. 'I'm not going to try to spoil things for you. I just want to see you happy.' His face grew serious. 'Don't make the same mistakes I did. I held back because I was always looking for something better that might come along. And I'll always regret losing your mum.'

Kieran folded his arms. 'She's been happy with Martyn, and they love each other.'

'I know, and I'm glad. I'm not going to try muscling in,' Tom said softly. 'She deserves a decent husband—someone who'll treat her properly, the way I never did. Was Martyn good to you?'

'Yes. You know my name's Bailey now—like his?'

Tom nodded. 'I wasn't going to sign the forms. Then your mum pointed out that I'd made a right hash of being a dad and it was the best thing I could do for you, so you'd feel a real part of the family and not as if you were just a hanger-on with a different name. It took me a month or two to come round to her point of view, but I did the right thing in the end.'

Again, Kieran found himself lost for words. He hadn't expected this sort of honesty from Tom Galloway.

'I remarried six years ago. Maureen made me grow up. Well, it was about time I did—I'm sixty-two. I'm learning to be a better husband this time round.' He shrugged. 'She's got a couple of girls from her first marriage. I'm a stepgrandad now. I hope I'll make a better fist of being a grandad than I did of being a dad.' He paused. 'Do you want to see my grandchildren?'

Kieran suppressed the wave of resentment. Wasn't this supposed to be about *them*? Or maybe his father just wanted to show off his new life. Prove something. 'OK.'

Tom took a couple of photographs from his wallet and another, much older photograph fell out. Kieran picked it up and stared at it. He knew that face. Knew the puppy the little boy was hugging. Had ripped those trousers climbing a tree and had worn that T-shirt until it had been so full of holes that his mother had consigned it to the bin.

'That's me.'

'My little boy.' Tom's face was full of remorse. 'The one I let down, all those years ago. The one I wished I'd been there for.' He held his hand out for the photograph. 'But that's in the past. I can't change what happened.'

'No.' Kieran gave him back the photograph and took the others. 'These are your grandchildren?'

'Emily, Sophie and Olivia. Sue—that's Maureen's oldest—is six months pregnant with her second. But I think she's going to have a girl again.'

The longing on his face as he spoke told Kieran that Tom desperately wanted a grandson. A grandson he could spoil and play football with and teach to ride a bike. To make up for the son he'd lost, maybe?

'Do you live around here?' Kieran asked.

Tom nodded. 'So does Sue. She's booked in to have the baby at your place, actually. Though I didn't see you there when Olivia was born last year.'

'I was at the Hampstead Free until this year,' Kieran explained.

'Oh. So you live in West London?'

Kieran grinned. 'Hardly. I don't think many people can afford a place in Hampstead nowadays! Anyway, I like East London. I've got a two-bed terrace—nothing fancy, but it's big enough for me, Tess and Charlie.'

Tom blinked. 'You've got a son?'

'A nephew,' Kieran corrected. 'Tess is my baby sister. She's staying with me for a while.'

'I had no idea. But, then, why would I? We're strangers,' Tom said.

'Yes.'

'Nothing like each other. I'm retired now, but I never went that high up the ladder when I worked. You're a high flyer. You could go anywhere you choose, do anything you want to.'

True. But what he really wanted was to settle down. With Jude.

If she'd have him.

'So you're going to be a professor one day?'

'Maybe.'

Tom sighed. 'This isn't going to work, is it? I said to Maureen after you phoned, "I'm going to see my son." She warned me not to expect too much. That just because you wanted to see me tonight, it didn't mean you wanted me to be part of your life. I know I made a mess of things— I spent too much time trying to prove things to myself instead of listening to you. But I've changed. I've learned that life's about more than what you look like or how many birds you can pull in an evening. It's about giving, not taking. I'm only sorry that I can't turn back the clock.'

Kieran stared at his father. The more he looked, the more he could see himself in Tom Galloway, from the dark eyes to the serious look on his face. He wasn't sure if that was a good thing or a bad one. But how would he ever know, unless he tried? 'But you can change the future,' he said softly.

Tom went very still. 'Are you saying you want to see me again after tonight?'

'Yes. I'd like to introduce you to the woman I love. The woman I nearly lost,' he added, more to himself.

'Why? You didn't…?'

'I didn't mess around with another woman, no.' Kieran took a deep breath. 'Though, if I'm honest, I thought I was like you were. Always thinking of myself and taking, not giving.'

Tom shook his head. 'No, you're not me. You're your own person. Don't let yourself be driven by my mistakes— and, heaven knows, I've made enough of them. If you love her and it feels right, hold onto her.' He grinned. 'Don't look so surprised.'

'I…' Kieran spread his hands. 'I didn't expect you to say something like that,' he admitted.

'I've learned a lot, Kieran. I've grown up. And if it won't upset your mum and you're happy to stay in touch with me, I'd like to see you again. Get to know you as a man, the way I never did when you were a boy. And maybe you could meet Maureen and the girls. I know it's not going to happen overnight, that it's going to take time for us to get to know each other again, and you might never feel you can call me anything but Tom—but I'd like to try.'

This time, Kieran thought, he could believe his father. 'Me, too.'

When Kieran left the White Horse, two hours later, he went straight to Judith's house. He didn't want to ring her first and risk her saying she didn't want to see him. And if she was out…well, he could wait. As from now, he had all the time in the world.

He rang the doorbell. There was no answer, and he was about to go and sit on the wall between the street and her garden and wait for her when the door opened.

'Kieran. I wasn't expecting to see you tonight.'

'I've been having a long-overdue talk. With my father.'

'Your father?' Her face showed shock.

'Can I come in?'

'I—uh—yes, sure.' She stood aside, then closed the door behind him. 'Coffee?'

'No. I just want to talk to you.'

She nodded. 'Come and sit down.' She picked the chair, he noticed, rather than the sofa. But then again, he'd hurt her badly. He couldn't expect her to fall straight into his arms—any more than Tom had expected Kieran to hug him and call him Dad.

'So how did it go?'

'Nothing like I'd expected. He looked just like anyone else's dad. He's changed, Jude. It's not like when I was little, when he had a quarter of an ear on me and the rest of his attention on working out who he was going to flirt with next. We talked. And he actually listened to me.'

'Are you going to see him again?'

'Yes. It's going to take time to heal all the old wounds, but we're going to give it a try. Maybe we can be friends this time round. Learn to accept each other for what we are.'

'Sounds good.'

'I think…' Kieran took a deep breath. 'I think we were both right about him. I'm not like he was—but he's like I want to be.'

'How do you mean?' Judith tipped her head on one side.

'He's settled. Married to a woman he loves. Actually, he gave me some good advice tonight. "If you love her and it feels right, hold onto her." I know who I am now and who I want to be.' He smiled at her. 'My name's Kieran Bailey and I've met the one woman I want to be with for the rest of my life. I'm not very good at trusting or letting people really close, but I'm willing to learn, if I can get her to teach me.' His smile faded. 'I love you, Jude. I want to grow old with you and raise children with you and run the best obstetrics department in London with you right by

my side. And I want a huge wedding. I want the whole
world to know I love you.'

Jude blinked hard. Had she just heard that right? Had
Kieran declared his love for her?

'Everything that happened after Tess took the overdose…I handled it badly. Really badly. And I've got no
excuses lined up, no glib words to help me worm my way
out of it. But I do know who I am. I'm not my father. I'm
me. I'm not perfect and I'm going to make stupid mistakes
in the future, so I can't promise you a perfect life—but I
can promise that I'll love, honour and cherish you for the
rest of our days.' His eyes were very dark, very intense.
'Will you give me a second chance?'

She wanted to believe him. She really, really wanted to
believe him. But supposing…?

He crossed the room and knelt at her feet. He took one
hand and raised it to his lips. 'If you need time to think
about it, I'll wait.'

She nodded. 'I need time.'

'No pressure.' He stroked her face. 'But I meant what I
said. I love you. And that's for always.'

Judith spent the next day walking around Kew Gardens,
thinking. Could she trust Kieran now? Would he let her in
for good—or would he push her away, the moment a crisis
loomed?

She still wasn't sure by the end of the week—a week
when he treated her as just another colleague at work, as
he'd promised, without putting pressure on her. She could
see the hope and longing in his eyes, but she just wasn't
ready to give him an answer—even after they'd worked
together on a difficult preterm delivery of IVF triplets,
when emotions had been running high and even Jan from
the special care unit had been in tears after they'd lost one.

'Well done. We saved two of them, thanks to you,' he whispered to her afterwards, sliding one arm round her shoulders and giving her a hug. 'And I notice you're not carrying your book around any more. So you believe in yourself, just as I believe in you.'

Yes. But did she believe enough in him?

Late on the Saturday night, when she was in bed, reading, her phone rang.

Who would ring her this late at night? Except—her heart speeded up—Kieran. Though he'd promised to give her all the time she wanted. 'Hello?' she said cautiously.

'Jude. Come to your window.'

'Kieran?' Was he outside? But if so, why didn't he just ring the doorbell? Why did he want her to go to the window?

'Just come to the window and open it, sweetheart,' he said softly.

Curiosity got the better of her. She dragged on her dressing-gown, pulled her curtains back, pushed up the bottom of the sash window and leaned out.

Then she blinked. Hard. Was it her imagination, or was Kieran *really* standing in her front garden, holding a cardboard cut-out guitar? He turned to fiddle with something on her wall. Moments later, the sound of Dire Straits filled her garden—and the rest of the street. 'Romeo and Juliet'. She blinked again as she saw what Kieran was doing. Pretending to play the guitar. Miming the words of the song to her. Blowing kisses to her window.

He was serenading her.

In the middle of the street.

In front of all her neighbours—including her best friend!

She saw the twitching curtains opposite and groaned. Oh, no. She was never, ever, ever going to live this down.

Particularly when the only time Kieran did sing—completely out of key—was when he changed 'Juliet' to 'Judith'. Making it quite clear that the song was especially for her.

She didn't know whether to laugh or cry or cringe. Kieran—who most definitely *couldn't* sing—was serenading her. Miming to one of the most romantic songs, one she'd loved as a teenager. Playing a cut-out guitar and not caring who heard as he declared his love for her.

Kieran, who usually kept his private life extremely private.

The song finished. He stopped the tape and dropped to one knee.

'I love you, Judith. Will you marry me?' he called.

He meant it. He really, really meant it.

'I'm coming down,' she said.

'Ju—'

She pulled the window down before he could say anything more. Ran downstairs and unlocked the front door. He was waiting for her on the doorstep. And then she was in his arms.

'I can't believe you did that,' she said, when he'd stopped kissing her and they were back inside her house with the door firmly shut. 'It's the soppiest... And you've got more of a tin ear than Zoe has!'

'Why do you think I mimed most of it?' he teased back.

'And a cardboard cut-out guitar...'

'I was going to get a real one. Tess found me looking through the phone directory to find a music shop. When I told her what I was planning, she made me a featherboard guitar. She did me a Mark Knopfler mask, actually, with a headband and everything—but I wanted you to know exactly who was serenading you.'

'Do you know how many curtains were twitching out there?'

He shrugged. 'There's only one pair that counted. Yours. Will you marry me, Jude?'

'You said you wanted a huge wedding. In a church?'

He nodded. 'Your choice.'

'And I can have as many bridesmaids as I want?'

'Yes.'

She smiled. 'Good. That's Zo, Holls and Tess. And Charlie as my ringbearer, in a white sailor suit.'

He grinned. 'It won't be white by the time he gets to the church, but yes.'

'And I don't have to walk down the aisle to Wagner?'

'You can walk down the aisle to anything you like,' he promised, 'as long as you walk down the aisle to me.'

'Beethoven's ''Ode to Joy'', then. Sung by a choir.' She hummed the first few bars.

'Are you going to put me out of my misery?' he demanded.

'What? We're talking wedding plans, aren't we?'

'You haven't officially agreed to marry me.' He rubbed his nose against hers. 'I'll make it easy for you. One word, three letters. Consonant, vowel, consonant. On the other hand, if you still need a bit of persuading, me, my tape deck and my featherboard guitar can run through the rest of our repertoire.'

Judith's jaw dropped. 'You were planning *other* songs?'

'Oh, yes. I've got a loaded tape deck. Ninety minutes' worth. So I could go out there and do the full concert, if you like. I mean, obviously, I'll be miming it. I can't reach Joni Mitchell's high notes on ''Case of You''. But I'll mean every word I mime.'

She leaned her forehead against him, laughing. 'Oh, Kieran. I really can't believe…'

'Believe in me,' he whispered, 'like I believe in you. Will you marry me?'

He loved her enough to do something mad and crazy and soppy and sweet, and not care who saw him. He loved her enough to serenade her. He loved her enough to believe in her.

And now she believed in him.

She straightened up and looked him in the eye. 'Yes.'

He punched the air, whooped, spun her round in a circle and kissed her.

The phone rang. They ignored it and let the answering-machine take the message.

'It's Holly. I can't stand the suspense. You have to tell me,' Judith's best friend begged. 'Did you say yes?'

Then Mrs Smith opposite rang, with the same question.

And Mr Freeman, the neighbour on the opposite side from Holly.

'They're all keyholders for my burglar alarm,' Judith muttered, her face growing hot.

'And they all want to know.' Kieran kissed her lightly and went to the door.

'What are you doing?' she squeaked.

He winked, opened the front door and leaned out. 'She said yes,' he called.

And closed the door again on the applause.

MILLS & BOON®

0205/03b

Live the emotion

_Medical romance™

THE DOCTOR'S PREGNANCY SURPRISE by Kate Hardy

(London City General)

Dr Holly Jones has never recovered from the shock of
losing David Neave's baby – nor from the way he
disappeared from her life. Years later they find
themselves working together in A&E, and as their long-
held secrets come bubbling to the surface they begin to
renew their very special bond. Until Holly discovers
she's pregnant again!

THE CONSULTANT'S SECRET SON by Joanna Neil

Dr Allie Russell is managing the best she can – juggling
her work in A&E and Search & Rescue with her two-
year-old son. Then Nathan Brewster arrives back in her
life as the new A&E consultant. He doesn't know he's
Matty's father, and Allie wants to keep it that way. But
as she and Nathan draw closer again, it's only a matter
of time before he discovers the truth!

NURSE IN RECOVERY by Dianne Drake

Charge nurse Anna Wells's life has been shattered by
an accident. She needs someone very dedicated and
special to help her put the pieces back together…
someone like brilliant Rehabilitation doctor Mitch
Durant. But Mitch is burnt out, the last thing he needs
is another patient – until he sees Anna and realises
she's a challenge he just has to take on…

On sale 4th March 2005

*Available at most branches of WHSmith, Tesco, ASDA, Martins,
Borders, Eason, Sainsbury's and all good paperback bookshops.*

Visit www.millsandboon.co.uk

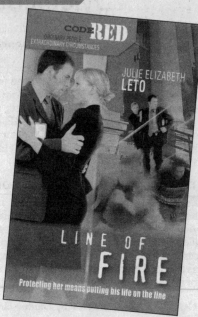

FREE

4 BOOKS AND A SURPRISE GIFT!

We would like to take this opportunity to thank you for reading this Mills & Boon® book by offering you the chance to take FOUR more specially selected titles from the Medical Romance™ series absolutely FREE! We're also making this offer to introduce you to the benefits of the Reader Service™—

> ★ **FREE home delivery**
> ★ **FREE gifts and competitions**
> ★ **FREE monthly Newsletter**
> ★ **Books available before they're in the shops**
> ★ **Exclusive Reader Service offers**

Accepting these FREE books and gift places you under no obligation to buy; you may cancel at any time, even after receiving your free shipment. Simply complete your details below and return the entire page to the address below. You don't even need a stamp!

YES! Please send me 4 free Medical Romance books and a surprise gift. I understand that unless you hear from me, I will receive 6 superb new titles every month for just £2.69 each, postage and packing free. I am under no obligation to purchase any books and may cancel my subscription at any time. The free books and gift will be mine to keep in any case.

M5ZEE

Ms/Mrs/Miss/Mr...Initials ....

BLOCK CAPITALS PLEASE

Surname ....

Address ....

....

....Postcode ....

Send this whole page to:

The Reader Service, FREEPOST CN81, Croydon, CR9 3WZ

Offer valid in UK only and is not available to current Reader Service™ subscribers to this series. Overseas and Eire please write for details. We reserve the right to refuse an application and applicants must be aged 18 years or over. Only one application per household. Terms and prices subject to change without notice. Offer expires 31st May 2005. As a result of this application, you may receive offers from Harlequin Mills & Boon and other carefully selected companies. If you would prefer not to share in this opportunity please write to The Data Manager at PO Box 676, Richmond, TW9 1WU.

Mills & Boon® is a registered trademark owned by Harlequin Mills & Boon Limited.
Medical Romance™ is being used as a trademark. The Reader Service™ is being used as a trademark.

WIN a romantic weekend in PARiS

To celebrate Valentine's Day we are offering you the chance to WIN one of 3 romantic weekend breaks to Paris.

Imagine you're in Paris; strolling down the Champs Elysées, pottering through the Latin Quarter or taking an evening cruise down the Seine. Whatever your mood, Paris has something to offer everyone.

For your chance to make this dream a reality simply enter this prize draw by filling in the entry form below:

Name _____

Address _____

_____Tel no: _____

Closing date for entries is 30th June 2005

Please send your entry to:

**Valentine's Day Prize Draw
PO Box 676, Richmond, Surrey, TW9 1WU**

Terms and Conditions

1. Draw open to all residents of the UK and Eire aged 18 and over. No purchase necessary. To obtain a copy of the entry form please write to the address above. All requests for entry forms from this address must be received by 31st May 2005. One entry per household only. 2. The offer is for one of three prizes of two nights free accommodation in Paris for two adults sharing a twin or double room and based on flights and accommodation being booked as a package. Flights cannot be booked separately or arranged through any other travel company or agent, and are dependent on availability. Holiday must be taken by 31st December 2005. Restrictions on travel may apply. 3. No alternatives to the prize will be offered. 4. Employees and immediate family members of Harlequin Mills & Boon Ltd are not eligible. 5. To be eligible, all entries must be received by 30th June 2005. 6. No responsibility can be accepted for entries that are lost, delayed or damaged in the post. 7. Proof of postage cannot be accepted as proof of delivery. 8. Winners will be determined in a random and independently supervised draw from all eligible entries received. 9. Prize winner notification will be made by letter no later than 14 days after the deadline for entry. 10. If any prize or prize notification is returned as undeliverable, an alternative winner will be drawn from eligible entries. 11. Names of competition winners are available on request. 12. As a result of this application you may receive offers from Harlequin Mills & Boon Ltd. If you do not wish to share in this opportunity, please write to the data manager at the address shown above. 13. Rules available on request.